A S

Animal Farm

Nigel Bryant

*(with humble acknowledgements
to George Orwell)*

Nigel Bryant has asserted the right under Copyright, Designs and Patents Act 1988 to be identified as the author of this work.

Nigel Bryant
1 December 2013

ISBN: 978-1-291-69053-8

PublishNation, London
www.publishnation.co.uk

Prologue

Benjamin, the old and quiet donkey, thought about what had happened on Manor Farm whilst he was walking back to his stall. It started a long time ago. Old Major, the prize Middle White boar, had called all the animals together in the barn to announce that he had a vision and that the animals could be free. The Old Major called his vision Animalism. After his talk, the animals sang the anthem "Beasts of England" which begins:

> Beasts of England, beasts of Ireland,
> Beasts of every land and clime,
> Hearken to my joyful tidings
> Of the golden future time.
> Soon or late the day is coming,
> Tyrant Man shall be o'erthrown,
> And the fruitful fields of England
> Shall be trod by beasts alone.

Then they all went to bed thinking about what could happen. Four days later the Old Major died. The idea lived on particularly in the minds of the pigs that were far more intelligent than the rest of the animals. The only exception perhaps was Benjamin. He was the oldest animal on the farm, and the worst tempered. He seldom talked and never laughed. Benjamin was devoted to Boxer, the cart horse; the two of them usually spent their

Sundays together in the small paddock beyond the orchard, grazing side by side and never speaking.

Manor Farm was owned by Mr. and Mrs. Jones. One Saturday Mr. Jones had gone out drinking as usual and did not return until Sunday lunchtime. The farm hands had all gone out hunting rabbits and had neglected to feed the animals. When Mr. Jones returned the animals gathered together; the years of frustration and maltreatment had built up into an irresistible force. They drove Mr. Jones off the farm. Mrs Jones was a middle aged, stocky woman. When she heard what had happened to Mr. Jones, she threw a few clothes into an old, battered suitcase and left the farmhouse. She ran or, rather, waddled down the lane carrying the suitcase in one hand and waving the other frantically. She alternately cried and howled, screaming abuse at the animals. She was followed quickly by Moses, the tame raven. Sometime later, Mr. Jones died whilst resident in a Home for the Inebriated.

The animals were amazed at how easily the rebellion succeeded. They renamed the farm 'Animal Farm'. The pigs soon emerged as leaders. They taught themselves to read and write and they took responsibility for planning and making decisions. All the animals learnt to read to varying degrees. Muriel, the white goat, could read fairly fluently, taking the time to read old newspapers to the other animals. Boxer, the cart horse, could not get beyond the letter D. Standing at 18 hands high, Boxer's contribution to the farm was his immense strength and dedication. His partner was Clover, a stout motherly mare approaching middle life, who had never quite got her figure back after her fourth foal.

There were three leaders amongst the pigs. Napoleon was a large, rather fierce-looking Berkshire boar, the only Berkshire on the farm, not much of a talker, but with a reputation for getting his own way. Snowball was a more vivacious pig than Napoleon, quicker in speech and more inventive, but was not considered to have the same depth of character. Squealer was a small fat pig with very round cheeks, twinkling eyes, nimble movements, and a shrill voice. He was a brilliant talker. The pigs created a list of laws that were painted on the end of the barn:

The Seven Commandments

1. Whatever goes upon two legs is an enemy.
2. Whatever goes upon four legs, or has wings, is a friend.
3. No animal shall wear clothes.
4. No animal shall sleep in a bed.
5. No animal shall drink alcohol.
6. No animal shall kill any other animal.
7. All animals are equal.

Minimus, a pig with a talent for writing poetry and songs, wrote an ode to Napoleon which began:

> Friend of fatherless!
> Fountain of happiness!
> Lord of the swill-bucket! Oh, how my soul is on
> Fire when I gaze at thy
> Calm and commanding eye,
> Like the sun in the sky,
> Comrade Napoleon!

Napoleon approved of this poem and it was inscribed on the wall of the big barn, at the opposite end from the Seven Commandments. It was surmounted by a portrait of Napoleon, in profile, executed by Squealer in white paint.

Over the years the animals kept the farm going. They did not seem to work any less hard or have more food but the farm was theirs. The pigs continued to lead while the other animals did all the work. Squealer announced regularly that production was up, food supplies had increased, and wastage reduced.

Next door to Manor Farm was a farm named Foxwood. It was a large, neglected, old-fashioned farm with all its pastures worn out. The hedges were unkempt and straggly. Some hedges were overgrown and out of control whilst others were threadbare allowing animals to wander in and out as they pleased. Foxwood was owned by Mr. Pilkington, an easy-going gentleman farmer who spent most of his time fishing or hunting according to the season.

On the other side was a farm, called Pinchfield. It was smaller and better kept. Mr. Frederick, its owner, was a tough, shrewd man, perpetually involved in lawsuits and with a name for driving hard bargains. Mr. Pilkington and Mr. Frederick disliked each other so much that it was difficult for them to come to any agreement.

On Animal Farm there was a pile of timber which was to be sold to Mr. Pilkington but at the last moment the timber was instead sold to Mr. Frederick. The animals were surprised by this alliance with what they considered to be an unfriendly neighbour. They listened to Boxer who always said "Napoleon knows best". The animals had no bank account and Mr. Frederick paid cash which Napoleon proudly showed to the animals. Mr. Whymper, a solicitor and the pigs' contact with the outside world, took the cash into the local town, Willingdon. When he returned, he reported that the notes were forgeries. Resentment against Mr. Frederick grew.

In the long pasture there was a small knoll which was the highest point on the farm. Snowball declared that this was just the place for a windmill, which could be made to operate a dynamo and supply the farm with electrical power. This would bring light to stalls and warm them in the winter. The electricity could also run the farm machinery. Snowball occupied an empty shed and using books that he had taken from the farmhouse he worked hard for three weeks to develop the plans for the windmill. Napoleon opposed the building of a windmill saying they should focus on the farm and its production. Eventually Snowball emerged with completed plans. After going through the project, savage dogs trained by Napoleon chased Snowball off the farm and he was never seen again. The animals thought that that was the end of the windmill but Napoleon announced he had plans for a new windmill and it had been his idea all along.

The animals started building. They used limestone that was freely available on the farm but it came in large pieces. They dragged the stone with desperate slowness up the slope to the top of the quarry, where they were toppled over the edge, to shatter in smaller pieces below. This was a long, hard process. They struggled for months collecting enough stone to build the windmill. The hardest worker was Boxer who got up thirty minutes earlier to put in a full day's work moving stones. Eventually the building was completed. Unfortunately one evening there was a tremendous storm and that blew the building down. Subsequently Squealer announced that the demolition was an act of sabotage by the outcast Snowball.

The animals determined to build a bigger, stronger windmill. They worked hard for months and eventually the building was completed. The walls were twice as thick so no storm could demolish it. One day Mr. Frederick and his men invaded the farm, attacked the animals and took control of the windmill. The animals thought that Mr. Frederick could not harm the windmill but his men planted dynamite and blew it up into thousands of pieces. The animals were so enraged that they counter attacked and drove Mr. Frederick and his men from Animal Farm.

Despite the setbacks, the windmill was built eventually. It did not provide creature comforts for the animals but was used to grind corn for Animal Farm and other farms, generating some income.

Over the years the pigs contravened the seven Commandments. These were painted over one by one as they were broken by the pigs. What remained was one commandment:

'all animals are equal but some are more equal than others'

Napoleon, Squealer and the others took to living in the house, sleeping on the beds, wearing clothes, and drinking beer. They were protected and their orders enforced by the group of loyal, ferocious dogs who had been brought up to be totally obedient to Napoleon. These dogs destroyed all animals that had opposed Napoleon's orders; four pigs, three hens, three sheep, a goose, and several others.

At the weekly Sunday meeting following the executions, Squealer announced that the rebellion was complete. The animals need no longer sing 'Beasts of England'. In its place, Minimus, the pig poet, had composed another song which began:

'Animal Farm, Animal Farm, Never through me shalt thou come to harm!'

'Beasts of England' was heard no more on Animal Farm. However, since the rebellion the pigeons had been travelling far and wide to other farms teaching the animals they met the words of 'Beasts of England'. Thus the words and spirit of the anthem were not lost completely. Finally, Napoleon decreed that the farm would revert to its original name – 'Manor Farm'.

One evening, the animals could hear a lot of noise coming from the farmhouse. They crept up to the windows and looked inside.

"There was the same hearty cheering as before, and the mugs were emptied to the dregs. But as the animals outside gazed at the scene, it seemed to them that some strange thing was happening. What was it that had altered in the faces of the pigs? Clover's old dim eyes flitted from one face to another. Some of them had five chins, some had four, some had three. But what was it that seemed to be melting and changing? Then, the applause having come to an end, the company took up their cards and continued the game that had been interrupted, and the animals crept silently away.

But they had not gone twenty yards when they stopped short. An uproar of voices was coming from the farmhouse. They rushed back and looked through the window again. Yes, a violent quarrel was in progress. There were shoutings, bangings on the table, sharp suspicious glances, furious denials. The source of the trouble appeared to be that Napoleon and Mr. Pilkington had each played an ace of spades simultaneously.

Twelve voices were shouting in anger, and they were all alike. No question, now, what had happened to the faces of the pigs. The creatures outside looked from pig to man, and from man to pig, and from pig to man again; but already it was impossible to say which was which."

The animals stared through the window of the farmhouse with strange feelings. Not having the intelligence of the pigs they were not sure what they were seeing. They felt confused, threatened, betrayed but were not able to put into words the emotions that they felt. It was impossible to tell the pigs from the humans. Napoleon could be the brother of the farmer Pilkington. The animals stood in silence. Then to break the silence Clover, tired and weary, said 'remember what Boxer used to say "Napoleon is always right".' At this the animals, or lower animals as they were now known, started to walk away. Clover, the mare, followed by Benjamin, the donkey, Muriel the white goat, the sheep and the cows went slowly to their stalls and resting places. Moses, the tame raven, who had returned to the farm, flew overhead and then settled on his perch by the back door.

But that night none of the animals were settled. Each animal tried to work out what was wrong. Had the pigs always looked like humans? Had they always behaved like humans? The animals shifted from hoof to hoof or leg to leg trying to get comfortable and sleep for the night but nobody slept well that night. The following morning they woke up to discover that not much had really changed. Manor Farm, which for a brief time had been known as Animal Farm, carried on in much the same way. The pigs looked like humans but inside they had not changed. The pigs lived inside the farmhouse and very rarely came out to see the lower animals. The animals continued with their business around the farm. With winter setting in, it grew colder; food was scarce and the animals vaguely remembered that it had been better but couldn't be sure.

Chapter I

Eventually the spring came.

The days grew longer and warmer. The animals felt relieved that they had survived the winter. Although they were getting older and feeling their age the long-standing members of the farm were still hanging on. After a while, spring started to turn to summer; the days were even longer. The weather turned hotter and drier; the animals did not know whether they preferred shivering in the cold or suffering in the heat. The pigs staying inside the farmhouse were not bothered at all by changes in the weather. The animals hoped that the hot dry spell would end soon. Tempers were short. They started bickering with each other; cows argued with sheep; sheep argued with ducks; ducks argued with hens.

The hot weather affected the animals and the farm itself. The heat dried out the wood and paint of the buildings, and the timber started to crack. The roof of one of the hen houses cracked and disintegrated leaving half the house exposed to the elements. The same was true for part of the barn. It dried out, splintered and, eventually, parts of the roof fell away. This was true for the other outbuildings and fences. Only the farmhouse was not affected because it was built with stone, brick and slate.

Then the weather started to change. The first sign was the insects flying lower and lower. The insects were followed by the swallows. They had been flying at great heights soaring in the clear hazy blue sky. Now they were coming within almost touching distance of the land so that they could catch insects. The woodpecker pecked fiercely and made calling noises. Then the cows, not the brightest of animals, felt that something was going to happen. They said they could feel something in their ears telling them that the weather will change. One particularly hot day the animals were standing around trying to keep cool when clouds started to form in the sky. Soon the sky was full of clouds which got darker and darker. Then the rain started. It began softly but became more and more severe. Soon it was torrential rain that none of the animals had ever seen before. The animals took shelter in the barn. They huddled together, sighing and shivering. Through the night the rain kept on relentlessly.

The younger animals were frightened. The older animals said that everything would be okay; they remembered storms like this from long ago. They did not last long and everything would be better tomorrow. The following day the awful weather continued. The rain hammered down on the corrugated tin roof of the barn. The wind threatened to blow the shutters and doors from their hinges. The animals huddled together in the barn occasionally foraging for food as best they could.

Of course, the pigs were comfortable. They gathered in the farmhouse and shut the door. They had enough food and provisions to last them through the duration of the storm. They listened to the weather forecast on the wireless. The storm covered not only their farm but also the county and most of the country. It was the worst recorded storm for 30 years. After two days of the storm the pigs started to run out of wood which was keeping their fire going night and day. They selected one of the dogs and told him to go to the barn and instruct the animals that they must collect wood. After delivering the message the dog managed to get back to the farmhouse wet, cold, bedraggled, but still alive. The animals were frightened that the dog would return with some of his friends and attack them. They decided that they would have to collect wood for the pigs. The sheep, believing that the pigs knew best, volunteered to go around the farmyard and collect dry wood from the stack yard. Despite the incessant wind and rain the sheep managed to collect enough wood to satisfy the pigs. But on the last journey from the stack yard to the farmhouse lightning struck an outbuilding which collapsed killing two of the sheep. The remaining sheep left the wood and hurried back to the barn. They told the other animals what had happened. Although there was a great feeling of sadness, the animals in the barn were too scared to go outside in the violent storm. The bodies of the two dead sheep were left in the yard. The pigs, indoors, warm and cosy, were not bothered at all by the dead bodies.

Moses, the tame raven, had been Mr. Jones's special pet. When the Old Major gave his talk to the animals before the rebellion, Moses claimed to know of the existence of a mysterious country called Sugarcandy Mountain, to which all animals went when they died. It was situated somewhere up in the sky, a little distance beyond the clouds, Moses said. In Sugarcandy Mountain it was Sunday seven days a week, clover was in season all the year round, and lump sugar and linseed cake grew on the hedges. During the storm, Moses had left his perch by the back door of the farm house and taken refuge in the barn along with all the other animals. The animals hated Moses because he told tales and did no work, but the thought of Sugarcandy Mountain gave some comfort to the animals especially the sheep. Benjamin, the donkey that usually said very little, muttered that Sugarcandy Mountain was nonsense and Moses should keep quiet and not put silly ideas into the heads of the animals. Nonetheless, Moses continued to caw about this dream world and the animals listened.

The following day the storm seemed to ease. The wind died down a little and the rain softened. The noise lessened and the animals started to feel that the end the storm was in sight. They began to feel that they could venture outside. Whilst they were considering late afternoon whether or not to go outside, the wind started up again. It grew stronger and stronger than the rain started to lash down even more fiercely than it had done before. The animals became very frightened. The sheep started bleating," What will become of us? What will become of us?" Even the older animals that had been through storms before began to wonder if they would survive this storm.

As evening wore on, the storm got stronger and stronger. The rain thrashed against sides, roof and doors. The wind with tremendous noise seemed to be about to blow down the barn. Then there was an almighty crash as the wind finally took hold of the barn doors and they swung open. All the animals started to panic but Muriel the most intelligent of the animals quickly realised what was happening and called all the animals to help close the doors. All the animals from the largest to the smallest pushed hard against the doors to close them against the ferocious wind. Once the doors were closed, the animals knew that something more permanent had to be arranged. They could not keep pushing against the doors forever. Muriel suggested that they needed some sort of strong props to hold the door closed and all the animals readily agreed. Most of the timber in the yard had been sold to Mr. Frederick but there was some timber left. Muriel thought there would be enough to create a sturdy enough barricade to block the door and save the animals from certain death if the storm did break through. The animals had to decide who would go out into the storm to collect the timber. There needed to be little discussion. The size of the timber meant that only the largest and strongest animals could possibly move it. The horses volunteered to collect the timber. Clover volunteered but it was agreed that she was too old and weak to contribute and, anyway, she was a comfort to a lot of the smaller animals in the barn.

The animals devised the plan. On the count of three, Muriel and Clover opened the door of the barn enough for the three horses to bolt out into the storm. They met the wind head on and had to bow their heads low to try and work their way through the howling wind and the rain. Once into the farmyard, Muriel and Clover tried to close the doors behind them. Again all the animals pushed as hard as they could against the doors until they finally closed them. The horses struggled to get to the timber but eventually they managed to carry enough timber back to start barricading the barn doors. They left the timber outside the doors for the time being and went back for another load. It was a long, hard struggle but eventually they managed to get back to the barn with a second load of timber. They decided that one more load would be enough and went back to the timber for the final load. By straining every muscle and using every last ounce of energy they managed to carry it back to the barn door. The horses told the animals inside the barn that they were back. Muriel and Clover opened the door enough for the horses to come through one at a time bringing timber with them. After the third load was safely inside the barn, the animals once more heaved and pushed to close the barn door. When it was closed, they built a makeshift barricade using the timber brought by the horses. This was enough to keep the barn doors closed and to keep the animals safe inside. But the cost was high. The three horses were cold wet and exhausted. The horses went into one corner of the barn and lay down to rest. But the strain of battling through the storm and carrying the timber was too much for them. The three horses died from exposure to the cold. There was little the animals could do but leave the bodies where they lay.

The storm continued day after day. The cows could sense no end to it. Day and night, night and day, the wind and rain kept up relentlessly. After five days, food was becoming scarce. The animals were becoming weaker and there seemed to be no end in sight. On the sixth day, Clover dared to look out through one of the shutters and thought the rain was slowing. The sky, which for six days had been deep black and purple, was brightening. Patches of sunshine started to appear. The rain stopped completely and the sky became a beautiful blue canopy once more.

The animals started to leave the barn with trepidation at first but then with increasing confidence. Then they could see the amount of damage that had been done. The first task was to bury the sad bodies of the two dead sheep. The pigs were going to throw the bodies into a corner of the farm and let them rot. The other animals insisted that the sheep were buried with some degree of dignity. After digging a hole in the orchard the two bodies were laid to rest. Muriel spoke softly and quietly:

"We have endured the worst storm in living memory. Most of us have survived; bruised and battered but still here. Sadly two of the sheep passed away. They were there at the rebellion; they have been by our sides through all our trials and tribulations. They were our friends and comrades. It is tragic that they have been taken from us. We will miss them. We will also remember the three horses who gave their lives. They worked valiantly so that the rest of us animals would be secure in the barn. We will miss them"

Following her eulogy, Muriel walked back to the barn. The other animals followed in silence, each thinking about events over the last few days.

But there was lots of work to do. The hen houses already damaged by the prolonged dry heat were now almost destroyed by the wind and rain. Of the three hen houses, only one remained in reasonable enough condition for the hens to return. Other buildings like the grain store and the potatoes store had been damaged. Buildings had been demolished; food supplies contaminated and muddy water was everywhere. Once it was clear that the storm had passed the pigs and dogs left the farmhouse. The pigs hesitated. They usually knew what to say and what to do. They immediately started giving instructions to the animals but these were vague. The animals started the clean-up process but without commitment or direction. The following day a van arrived to remove the bodies of the horses. Napoleon decreed that the sheep and horses would be remembered each February on Storm Day.

Napoleon ordered that any animal that was able to help the pigs but had refused would be eliminated by the dogs. Frightened for their own lives the hens declared that two of the sheep had refused to go out into the storm and collect wood. The two sheep were led off by the dogs and never seen again.

It would be a long time before Manor Farm started to look anything like it used to.

Chapter II

The storm had taken its toll not just on Manor Farm but also the two adjoining farms: Foxwood and Pinchfield. Farms further afield were also damaged. Beyond Pinchfield was a farm called Beech Tree Farm which was wealthy and well-maintained. Even Beech Tree had been affected by the ravaging wind and rain. Perhaps the most affected was Pinchfield. The storm seemed to hit this farm from both directions. Having recovered from violent wind and rain from the west, the storm changed direction and hit the farm from the east. The storm damaged livestock and buildings. Many of the outhouses were built of timber and not substantial enough to survive the howling gales. They were destroyed by the strong winds. This left little room for all the animals to gather and shelter. Several of the animals, including cows, sheep and hens lost their lives whilst trying to find shelter. The storm left the farm crippled and Mr. Frederick a shadow of his former self. At the end of the storm Mr. Frederick took to his bed.

Napoleon and the pigs on Manor Farm thought about the land and buildings on Pinchfield Farm. They were enemies of Mr. Frederick who, in the past, had given them fake banknotes in exchange for timber. This was just one of the events that contributed to the ill feeling between

Manor Farm and Pinchfield Farm. Before the great storm, Mr. Frederick had invaded their farm in an attempt to take possession. Mr. Frederick and his men had got as far as the windmill and whilst the animals of Manor Farm thought that it was indestructible, Mr. Frederick and his men had blown up the windmill using dynamite that they had brought with them. Napoleon and the pigs saw that Pinchfield was in a ravaged state and Mr. Frederick was ill and in no position to put up any fight. Napoleon decided that they would reverse the process and take Pinchfield into their possession.

Napoleon called a meeting of the pigs, helped by Mr. Pilkington and some of the men from Foxwood Farm. They plotted to take over Pinchfield Farm. The conspirators knew that on the farm were Mr. Frederick and several farm workers who owned weapons including shotguns. These workers kept an eye on Manor Farm because of the problems they had in the past. It would be difficult to mount a surprise attack. Likewise, it would be difficult to mount an all-out attack because of the number of workers and the weapons they possessed. Nonetheless, Napoleon was determined that they would take over Pinchfield farm in restitution for the damage caused by Mr. Frederick in the past. Franco and his group decided that they would attack Pinchfield Farm, very early on

Saturday morning at first light. They hoped that this would give them the element of surprise.

Meanwhile Mr. Verity the owner of Beech Tree Farm was thinking about Pinchfield Farm. He had also had problems with Mr. Frederick in the past. Mr. Verity decided that it would be fitting and just for him to take over Pinchfield. He called together his workers and told them that this was an ideal opportunity to take control of Pinchfield Farm so that they would not have to worry about any threats from that direction in the future. Like Napoleon, Mr. Verity was concerned that the Pinchfield workers would take up arms against his workers. However, he knew that Mr. Frederick was unwell and had taken to his bed. He decided that a surprise attack early in the morning would give them the best chance of taking Pinchfield Farm with the least casualties.

On the Saturday following the end of the great storm, both Napoleon and Mr. Verity invaded Pinchfield Farm. The workers on Pinchfield were helpless. They had no leadership and no real commitment to Mr. Frederick or the farm. All they could see for the months ahead were the difficulties of trying to rebuild the farm with little money, few resources and little food. Some even welcomed the advance of Manor Farm and Beech Tree Farm. Advancing from different directions the two opposing forces would meet in the middle of the farm. Napoleon, the pigs, Mr. Pilkington and some of his men had taken over almost half the farm including the main farmhouse when they met up with Mr. Verity and his men who had taken the barns, stables and the fields adjacent to Beech Tree Farm.

Mr. Frederick's workers told him that Napoleon and Mr. Verity were advancing into Pinchfield Farm. Mr. Frederick told his workers that they should put up a fight to the very end against these invaders. They told him it was pointless. They were tired, hungry and ill-prepared to fight. They knew that they had lost the farm to Napoleon and Mr. Verity, but Mr. Frederick was reluctant to admit defeat. When Napoleon with Mr. Pilkington and the pigs and men from their farms approached the outside of the farmhouse even Mr. Frederick recognised that the end was in sight. He died from sheer exhaustion.

The two opposing sets of invaders stood looking at each other like two large hay carts facing each other on a country lane. The immediate reaction of Napoleon was to fight Mr. Verity and his men but, unusually, he thought first before he decided to take any action. Rather than risk his own neck he would offer to talk to Mr. Verity in an attempt to reach a reasonable solution. Then sometime later when he wasn't in the line of fire he could take over the remainder of Pinchfield Farm.

Following this plan he invited Mr. Verity to meet and discuss the ownership of Pinchfield. The two went quietly to one side leaving the others still standing and staring at each other in confrontation.

Napoleon opened the conversation by saying that Mr. Frederick had caused great damage to Manor Farm and, indeed, the animals on Manor Farm and, therefore, Napoleon and the pigs should have control of the whole of Pinchfield. Mr. Verity countered by saying that he, his farm, and his men had suffered at the hands of Mr. Frederick and therefore had an equal right to the land and buildings of Pinchfield.

Mr. Verity continued by arguing the land and farm should belong to the descendants of Mr. Frederick, if they existed, and therefore any permanent ownership was out of the question. Mr. Verity wanted to manage the farm in the absence of identified inheritors until such time that the farm could become self-managed and autonomous. Once more this was clearly at odds with Napoleon who felt that the injustices carried out by Mr. Frederick entitled him and the pigs to take control forever.

It became clear that there was no easy solution to the problem of ownership. Finally, Mr. Verity proposed that the farm could be divided between Manor Farm and Beech Tree Farm according to the land currently held by both parties. Napoleon thought about this idea and quickly realised that this was the only realistic solution. He could take over half the farm, including the farmhouse, and think about acquiring the rest of the farm sometime in the future. Indeed he could complete the takeover of Pinchfield Farm and this would put him in a prime position for taking over Beech Tree Farm and beyond. So Napoleon agreed with Mr. Verity and reluctantly allowed him to shake his trotter.

To begin with all was well. The farm hands of Pinchfield were divided between Manor Farm workers and Beech Tree Farm workers. The Manor Farm workers were given accommodation in an outbuilding attached to the farmhouse. The Beech Tree Farm workers were housed in one of the outbuildings near the stables. Napoleon's occupation of the farmhouse in Pinchfield meant that the pigs had another building to inhabit.

As time went on, the differences of the two halves of Pinchfield started to become apparent. Mr. Verity who treated his staff fairly and gave them reasonable wages extended this approach to his newly acquired staff. The outbuilding that they occupied was upgraded to give warm, light, comfortable accommodation. They were well-fed and contented to work within the new regime.

On the other hand, the staff on Napoleon's side had to make do with poor accommodation, limited rations, and much maltreatment. They were expected to work with limited tools in all conditions - sun, rain, sleet, hail or snow. As the summer turned to autumn, it became clear that the Manor Farm side of Pinchfield was going to suffer more than the other. As the weather got worse the farm hands became more and more restless. Napoleon, fearing that the men would get together and create trouble, banned any collective meeting of more than two people. The simple pleasure of getting together as a group to play draughts or cribbage was prohibited. These rules were strictly enforced using the dogs as a deterrent. The workers were encouraged and rewarded for telling tales about each other.

Consequently rumours spread that the workers on the Manor Farm side of Pinchfield were going to down tools and cross over to work with Beech Tree Farm. Napoleon and the pigs, with help from Mr. Pilkington, had erected a wooden fence to mark the boundary between the two halves of the farm. It would be a simple matter crossing from one side to the other. However, the fence was patrolled by the dogs under the direction of Napoleon and the senior pigs. None of the farmhands crossed over because they knew what would happen. They would be savaged by the dogs whilst crossing over the fence or if they reached the other side, Napoleon in some way would get at them.

As time went on, the pigs became more anxious about being so close to their rivals. They decided that they would increase the height of the fence which separated the two halves of the farm. The fence was then extended to include the perimeter of Manor Farm itself. It was impossible for any animal or human to enter or leave Manor Farm or the Pinchfield annex without going through the main gate in the fence which was patrolled and guarded by the dogs.

The construction of this fence led to rumours and stories about what went on inside. Were the animals being maltreated? Were the animals starving? Were the animals still alive? To counter these rumours, Squealer gave updates to all and sundry saying how wonderful life was on Manor Farm. The Farm continued to be a model example of Animalism and collective effort.

The animals on Manor Farm thought that life would be easier because they had the extended farm and another farmhouse. But this was not the case. The best farmhands on Pinchfield had run away soon after the division of the farm. This left the remnants of the farmhands, helped by the animals of Manor Farm and managed by the pigs. Life remained as arduous as ever.

Chapter III

A couple of years later the lower animals sensed
changes in the pigs. They had not seen Napoleon
for some time and there were rumours that he was
ill. Manor Farm was now run by Napoleon's
deputies. Very occasionally Napoleon would make
an appearance. He looked frail and weak supported
on each side by two of the pigs. And then Napoleon
wasn't seen for several days. The days became
weeks and eventually the pigs admitted that he had
died. Napoleon was to be given a hero's send-off.
All the animals were given time off work to
congregate in the yard. Clover drew up outside the
farmhouse pulling a cart. The coffin containing
Napoleon was carried out by six of the pigs. It was
a large oak coffin with brass handles and a polished
nameplate. Napoleon had ordered it especially by
before his death. The coffin was laid on the cart
and Clover pulled the cart through the yard and out
towards the orchard. The dogs walked alongside of
the cart which was followed by the pigs and then
the other animals. They were told to fall into line
and follow Napoleon on his last journey to rest in
the orchard.

When they reached the orchard, they
discovered that a large hole had been dug into
which the coffin was ceremoniously lowered.
Whilst this was happening Squealer started to give

lengthy speeches. He told the assembled animals that they were lucky to have had a leader like Napoleon. He was the best pig the world had ever seen and they would never see his like again. Napoleon single-handedly had chased off the Joneses and delivered the farm into the hands of the animals. During his glorious leadership Manor Farm had prospered showing the world what could be done when animals worked together under the leadership and guidance of someone like him. Napoleon had also built the windmill despite the sabotage of Snowball, had fought off Mr. Frederick and the workers from Pinchfield Farm and had continued his glorious leadership on Manor Farm. Then one of the pigs let off both barrels of the shot gun left by Mr. Jones in the old farm. The animals led by the pigs were encouraged to cheer. As ever, the sheep immediately fell into line bleating that "Napoleon was great! Napoleon was great!" This was followed by singing the song composed by Minimus, the pig poet, which began:

'Manor Farm, Manor Farm,
Never through me shalt thou come to harm!'

Soon after, the pigs erected a statue of Napoleon on top of the burial mound. The pigs decreed that this had become a sacred place. Squealer announced that the day of Napoleon's funeral would be remembered each year as

Napoleon Day! The statue would be visited annually by the pigs and lower animals to pay homage to the great Napoleon.

Following the ceremony, the animals ambled back to the farmyard wondering what was in store. There were rumours of infighting and loud, bad tempered rows within the pigs. Eventually it was announced that the pigs had agreed a successor to Napoleon. This was to be Franco, another Berkshire boar, the pig who had acted as loyal deputy to Napoleon during the last illness troubled years of his life. Franco continued to run the farm in much the same way as Napoleon. Franco and the pigs maintained their hold on Manor Farm and Pinchfield Farm.

One Sunday the animals were instructed to meet together in the barn. Everybody came together half anxious, half confused by why they had been summoned. Once they were all gathered Franco made a majestic entrance followed by the rest of the pigs. As if rehearsed, the sheep bleated together. "Franco is great! Franco is great!" Franco mounted on the platform at one end of the barn and when the noise had subsided he started to speak. "Friends, I have something grave to tell you. Through the years we followed Napoleon and we thought that he was a great leader. However, I now have evidence that he was not the pig that we thought he was. He exaggerated his successes, took credit for anything that went right and blamed others for anything that went wrong. It saddens me to tell you this but we must be open and honest about our past mistakes. In the future Manor Farm will grow bigger and better." The animals were shocked and bewildered by this news. They had always believed that however hard things were, Napoleon knew best and that they were working along the right lines. Eventually life would become easier for them. Now they realised that this had been a myth and life was never going to get better, however, they felt that life under Franco could improve.

Over time Napoleon became more memory than fact. The annual celebration of Napoleon Day was cancelled and the animals celebrated Rebellion Day and Storm Day. The only pig to remember Napoleon was Squealer but one night Squealer disappeared. He was replaced by a pig loyal to Franco called Trumpet who continued to keep records so that he could prove that the farm was going from strength to strength. Like Squealer, Trumpet announced to the world that Manor Farm was efficient and productive. All the animals were thriving. However, the reality was that the animals still had a hard life with too much work and not enough food and comfort.

In the early years, Animal Farm had a strained relationship with the adjoining farms.

Eventually Napoleon developed a relationship with Mr. Pilkington of Foxwood Farm and this developed into a long-term friendship and working relationship. This was continued by Franco who befriended Mr. Pilkington and saw him as an ally and colleague. Mr. Pilkington's wife Gladys died soon after Franco replaced Napoleon as the head of Manor Farm. She left Mr. Pilkington with one son, Michael, and a daughter-in-law, Margaret.

One day Mr. Pilkington felt under the weather and took to his bed. He said he felt unwell and could not eat or drink. His temperature rose and finally the next day they called in the doctor who thought he had a severe bout of flu. He was tended by Margaret. She tried to give him bowls of soup and other food that she thought would nourish him; but he could eat very little. Meanwhile he maintained a high temperature and fever. Throughout the night he tossed and turned and got worse and worse. The following day they called in the doctor once more. He said that Mr. Pilkington should be kept calm and as comfortable as possible with cold wet flannels applied to his head. However, these did little to reduce his temperature. All through the night he was uncomfortable and his sleep was interrupted. Like the previous night he was hot, restless and his breathing became more and more difficult. Finally in the early hours of the morning he could breathe no more. Michael and

Margaret were saddened and concerned that they could not save him.

Over the years old Mr. Pilkington had run the farm virtually single-handed. He had little faith in Michael and delegated few tasks to him. Consequently Michael did not have a good working knowledge of how to run the farm. Whilst there were farmhands who had been around for what seemed like decades they just followed the orders of Mr. Pilkington. They were not given any responsibilities or the necessary skills to actually run the farm. Consequently the farm began to suffer. Tasks that should have been completed were started late or not at all; the fields were full of weeds; the animals neglected; the stores were starting to be depleted.

Whilst this was happening, Franco was keeping a close eye on the situation. He did not want the farm to fail completely and he recognised the opportunity to become more involved in its day-to-day running. He offered Michael and Margaret help and expertise in running the farm. They hesitated not wishing to relinquish what they thought was their autonomous control. Before they could finish their deliberations, Franco sent a group of pigs supported by a handful of dogs to Foxwood Farm where they took up residence. Within days the pigs had established full control of the farm.

The dogs were there as a reminder about who was now in charge.

In addition to the Pilkington family, the farm employed a handful of staff. All but one of these fled to neighbouring farms rather than remain on the farm run by the pigs. The one remaining farmhand was too old and frail to change his lifetime habits.

The pigs installed themselves on Foxwood Farm. Having got used to a standard of living in Manor Farm, they made themselves comfortable in the farmhouse. Michael and Margaret Pilkington were allowed to keep one bedroom but the rest of the house was taken over by the pigs. Many years before, there had been a command "no animal would sleep in a bed". This command had long since been broken and amended to "no animal should sleep in a bed with sheets". Other commands like "animals shall not drink alcohol at all" had also been abandoned long ago. The pigs ate and drank as they wished. They occupied most of the bedrooms and all of the ground floor. Michael and Margaret felt betrayed but there was little they could do but live side-by-side with the pigs and the dogs.

The farm was not mechanised. Consequently, the work had to be undertaken by the Foxwood animals whose workload increased considerably. They had heard from Squealer and Trumpet that life on Manor Farm was good, food was plentiful and weekends were relaxing. They soon discovered the harsh truth that they would be expected to work hard to provide for the Pilkingtons and to provide for the pigs at Manor Farm.

A few of the animals fled to friendly neighbouring farms such as Beech Tree. However, the dogs made sure that this was a rare occurrence. Franco decided that Foxwood would become part of Manor Farm. The fence that surrounded Manor Farm was extended to include Foxwood. However, there was no free access between Foxwood and Manor Farm. Dogs on both sides of the fence made sure that the animals on each farm stayed within their own space. Whilst the dogs were patrolling other animals, the sheep were coerced into spying for the pigs. They informed on any animal attempting to move from Foxwood to Manor Farm or vice versa. They also informed on any animal that was going to attempt to leave Foxwood or Manor Farm and go to the outside world. Any transgressions were dealt with quickly and savagely by the dogs. The animals in both Foxwood and Manor Farm were trapped with no means of escape and no means of improving their miserable lot.

Chapter IV

The following spring, Trumpet called together all the animals of Manor Farm. One Sunday morning, they gathered together in the barn. Trumpet marched proudly into the barn and stood on stage. He said with an air of satisfaction and pride that he could announce great news. In the past Manor Farm had invested very little in new equipment, Trumpet announced that this was going to change. In the last twelve months they had bought two spades, two forks, and two hoes. The investment in equipment was going to be multiplied a thousand fold. This was possible because of the wonderful management and financial acumen of the pigs. The animals were amazed by this news. How could they increase the implements by such a number? Did this mean that they would have 2000 spades, 2000 forks and 2000 hoes? Were they all going to be treated to new equipment to make life so much easier? Trumpet said at this point he would not go into detail but they should be aware that things were going to be change.

On the Wednesday following the meeting the animals woke up to the most horrendous noise in the farmyard. Their first thought was that the dreadful storm of years ago had returned. But it didn't sound like rain and thunder. It was too mechanical, too clanking, too noisy. It seemed to be just outside the barn. With one mind the animals staggered into the farmyard, blinking in the sunlight, to find out what was making all the noise. In the yard, they saw an enormous locomotive, almost as big as the barn. It was pulling an equally enormous trailer and on the trailer was a tractor. Workmen were busy placing ramps behind the trailer so that the tractor could be run down into the farmyard. Trumpet appeared and announced that the supremely clever Franco had bought a tractor that was 1000 times heavier and 1000 times more valuable than the tools they had purchased the previous year. Franco and the pigs had decided that their investment would be in one large one rather than a lot of small changes. The lower animals were not sure about the tractor. They would have preferred individual tools to make their lives easier. Anyway this was not a new, shiny, modern tractor; this was a second-hand tractor bought from a friend of the Pilkingtons.

The tractor was not shiny any more but it was very large and imposing. The front wheels were like the wheels on the car of Mr. Whymper, the solicitor. The rear wheels were enormous. The tyres stood as high as Clover which was the animals' measure of huge. Despite their concerns the animals were impressed.

The tractor was very basic with no screen or silencer. The noise it made when moving was deafening. Every so often there seem to be an explosion in the engine accompanied by a loud bang and the blast of black smoke through the exhaust pipe. But it was a tractor and Trumpet the pig could now claim that they had the first mechanised farm in the area. The animals were not allowed to drive the tractor. Only Franco and a few of the chosen pigs were allowed to drive it. Franco drove the tractor to show how important he was and never used it to do anything productive.

However, on one such occasion, Franco was driving the tractor around the perimeter of the farm when, half-way round, the tractor stalled. Franco attempted to start the tractor. It coughed and spluttered, but refused to start. Franco left it for a few minutes and tried to start the engine. Again the tractor refused to start. Franco tried for a long time to get it started without success. Eventually he sought help from Michael Pilkington. Although he knew little about farming he was good with engines. Michael Pilkington walked back with Franco to the tractor full of trepidation. He knew that if the tractor refused to start again he would be in deep trouble. When they reached the tractor it became obvious what the problem was. The lead from the key to the battery had come adrift. Trying to start the engine Franco had flooded it with diesel. Michael Pilkington tightened up the leads, waited for a while and then tried turning the key.

The tractor started once more. Franco drove back to the farm house and said nothing of the incident. From that day on Franco refused to drive the tractor. Thus if anything went wrong it would not be his fault. However, having tightened up the leads the tractor gave no more trouble. It was noisy and inefficient but at least it worked.

The animals wondered how the farm that was in dire straits could afford to buy even this old tractor. It soon became clear where the money was going to come from: more eggs taken from the hens, potatoes were taken from the store and grain was taken from the granary. Even a proportion of the milk which previously was monopolised by the pigs was put into churns and taken into the village for sale.

One impact of the arrival of the tractor was that Clover was taken off all but the lightest duties. By now Clover was getting on in years and it was all she could do to take Franco ceremoniously around the farm. This much reduced workload gave her a great sense of relief. She had been feeling exhausted at the end of each working day. Now she could get through the working day with some sense of achievement and look forward to the evenings when she could relax and try to remember happier days. However her semi-retirement was short lived. One evening when she was thinking about the old days and her partner Boxer, her heart stopped beating. The rest of the animals were very sad when the news spread around the farm. Most of the animals were not old enough to remember Clover as a young lively carthorse. Even fewer could remember Boxer. But when the van came to take away her body there was a general feeling of loss.

Each day the animals waited for a horse box to come to the farm with a replacement for Clover but no such horsebox came. The noisy, smelly tractor was put to work to do all of the jobs that Clover and Boxer used to do around the farm.

In addition to its practical duties on the farm, the tractor also became the centre of celebrations each year as Manor Farm celebrated Rebellion Day and Storm Day. It would lead a procession of all the animals around the farm starting at the barn, going to the orchard, around the windmill and going back to the farmhouse. At the front was the tractor pulling a trailer. On the trailer sitting resplendent in a large chair taken from the farmhouse was Franco looking very pleased with himself. The tractor was driven by a trusted pig not Franco himself who did not wish to drive the unreliable machine. The tractor and trailer were followed by the pigs marching; the pigs were followed by the dogs and behind the dogs came the lower animals.

Trumpet made sure that there was enough noise and singing so that the neighbouring farms,

Foxwood and Pinchfield, would be aware of the progression of the tractor and the animals. In fact the tractor made so much noise that the neighbouring farms could not help but know when it was moving. They were also aware when Rebellion Day and Storm Day occurred each year and expected to hear the cacophony of noise that accompanied the parades. The lower animals were not entirely sure about the purpose of the parades but they were pleased to get a welcome relief from working in the fields and anyway parading around the farm did no harm and kept them from getting into trouble with Franco and the pigs.

Whilst the parades were a good excuse to wander around the farm, what followed the parades was less welcome. Once they returned to the farmhouse, they would then gather in the barn. This was an occasion for Franco and Trumpet to tell them how splendid Manor Farm was doing, what wonderful management they got from Franco and the rest of the pigs, and how good their lives were. Most of the animals felt very uncomfortable not knowing how to respond to this self-aggrandising but the sheep as usual would bleat "Franco is great! Franco is great!" but the rest of the animals were still not so sure. They could live with Franco building up his own importance but occasionally he took the opportunity of the parade speech to denounce other farms such as Beech Tree and other people such as Mr. Verity. Franco also took the opportunity occasionally to denounce Napoleon whilst the sheep were bleating "Napoleon is bad! Franco is good!" The more intelligent animals were still confused by this message. How could the farm live for so long with a leader that was bad? And following this idea was Franco any better?

Each year the parades continued and the tractor took pride of place as the symbol of progress on Manor Farm.

Chapter V

Manor Farm was sandwiched between two other farms. On the one side was Foxwood Farm which had been annexed by Franco and the pigs. On the other side was Pinchfield Farm. After the great storm Pinchfield was divided up by Napoleon and Mr. Verity of Beech Tree Farm which lay beyond Pinchfield. After a few years Beech Tree Farm gave up its claim to Pinchfield and it had been handed over to a Mr. Lawrence who was a distant but friendly relative of Mr. Frederick the previous owner. The two halves of Pinchfield co-existed uneasily side by side. There was greater unease between Manor Farm and Beech Tree Farm. Franco would receive gossip from informants on Beech Tree Farm. Franco heard that Mr. Verity was amused by the outdated, noisy tractor that was being used on Manor Farm. Trumpet had told all the neighbours that Manor Farm was fully recognised mechanised and up-to-date but of course Mr. Verity knew differently.

Franco decided that he would improve the image of Manor Farm by making technological advancements. For thousands of years farming had been carried out in all weathers. Hot and cold, wet and windy, snow and sleet, it didn't matter because farming jobs had to be done. Generally they were labour-intensive, manual and backbreaking. Franco and the other pigs got together to discuss where they could improve the farming process. During the loud and often heated discussion several ideas were raised; each part of farming was considered. They could develop a seeding machine but they felt that seeding was the least difficult and onerous of the tasks on the farm. Then they considered that they could build a weeding machine. Creating the technology that would distinguish between weed and crops was considered to be beyond the capability of any of the pigs. So they moved on to think about harvesting. The one crop that was difficult to harvest was the potatoes each autumn because they were below ground. It was a particularly backbreaking task to go through the field, lifting the potato plants to see if any were still hanging on the plant itself and then digging through the soil to make sure that all the potatoes had been collected. The pigs decided that the one area where they could excel was potato picking. Franco declared that Manor Farm would produce a machine that would mechanically collect potatoes and reduce or get rid of all together the back-breaking task of potato picking.

In the past there had been an attempt to build a windmill. The pigs had acquired the relevant expertise and skills to complete this feat of building and engineering. Unfortunately the pig who planned and initially supervised the windmill was

Snowball. He had been perceived as a threat to Napoleon and had disappeared long ago. None of the existing pigs had any real planning, building, or engineering skills. Nonetheless, having been decreed by Franco, the pigs started to design a suitable machine that could be attached to the rear of the tractor. They were ordered to produce the machine to collect the potatoes during the following harvest in September.

The pigs decided that they needed one pig in charge. They chose a mature pig called Alfred who was reasonably intelligent and seemed to have some understanding of the engineering principles involved. In the past, they had built the windmill using books that they had found in the farmhouse. Alfred returned to these books to see whether they could help him with the difficult task of designing a potato picker. Of course, there was no direct equivalent in the old books previously owned by Mr. Jones. However, Alfred managed to fuse various ideas that had been used in the past for harrowing and sifting machines. Eventually he managed to draw a rough working plan of the proposed machine. Alfred then faced the problem of actually manufacturing the potato picker. They had no means on the farm of fabricating the necessary parts. Alfred talked with Mr. Whymper who had contacts that could make these parts.

Eventually, after much discussion and redrawing of the plans, the local blacksmith was given the task of producing the machinery. Payment was promised once the potatoes were harvested and sold in the local market. Several weeks later the first of the parts started to arrive at Manor farm. Alfred started to put the parts together as best he could. During the initial stages of assembly he realised that the picker would not work properly; the tolerances were too great and the parts would jam together. He redesigned the picker as best he could, and sent the new drawings via Mr. Whymper to the blacksmith. During the following weeks the new parts were delivered to Manor Farm.

Alfred and the other pigs set to work to put together the components to make a working machine. After much hammering and cursing the parts went together and the potato picker was completed. By now it was the end of August and the harvesting season was not far away. As soon as the flowers on the potatoes started to wilt, Franco said that it was time to harvest. Alfred connected the potato picker to the tractor, took his place on the seat of the ancient tractor and started the engine which at first wouldn't start. Alfred checked that all of the leads were connected and that there was diesel in the tank. He tried once more to start the engine. Again, it wouldn't start. Alfred became alarmed. He knew that Franco would not be at all pleased if the potato picker was not a tremendous success. He tried once more to start the tractor. After much cajoling, it started with a loud bang and the blast of black smoke from the exhaust pipe.

Alfred drove the tractor to the potato field and lined up the wheels with the troughs between the rows of potatoes. One of the other pigs lowered the picker into the soil at the beginning of the chosen row. Alfred put the tractor into gear, opened up the throttle and started to move. The combined noise of the tractor with the picker reminded the animals of the storm many years before. As the tractor lumbered forward, the picker churned its way along the row of potatoes. A few of the crop were thrown into the box at the back of the picker. Unfortunately a lot more potatoes were left on the ground and some were sliced into small pieces by the machine. The pigs told the other animals that they should follow the picker and collect the "few" missed by the machine.

During the following weeks the picker was put into service but with limited success. Potato picking remained a manual and backbreaking activity. Franco announced that the potato picker was a great success and a shining example of the technological advancements of Manor Farm. Trumpet spread the news as widely as he could that the Manor Farm potato picker was at the cutting edge of technology.

Next door at Pinchfield Farm Mr. Verity heard the announcements about the great success of the Manor Farm potato picker. However he also heard the rumour that the picker was less than successful. He decided that he would compete against Manor Farm and announced that he would produce a fully working potato picker by the following September. This news was initially conveyed to Franco but it soon spread throughout all the local farms that Mr. Verity had made this declaration.

Rather than attempt the project on his own, Mr. Verity enlisted the aid of an engineering company who specialised in farm equipment. Working with their top designer George Thomas, Mr. Verity produced specifications for what he wanted the machine to do. Mr. Thomas then created the plans and with the approval of Mr. Verity went back to the engineering company to build the machine. Producing the specifications took several weeks. This was followed by three months of planning so that the harvest in September was getting closer and closer. However Mr. Verity was determined that the machine would be ready for this year's harvest. In mid-July the plans were given to the engineering company with six weeks left to build and test the machine. Mr.

Verity was not a frivolous man and during the years at his farm he had amassed a reasonable amount of savings. He used some of this money to fund the engineers so that they could work day and night, seven days a week to produce the machine.

During the first week of September the machine was delivered to Beech Tree Farm. It was connected to the tractor and Mr. Verity took the machine for a test run. All seemed to be working perfectly. However the harvest was slightly late that year and several days of rain further delayed the collection. Eventually in the third week of September, the harvest was ready and the weather was suitable. Mr. Verity drove the tractor to his potato field, lined up with the first row potatoes and started moving slowly and steadily along the row. The farm hands had gathered to watch the inaugural run of the machine. As the tractor started to move, all the spectators held their breath. Then as the potatoes started to appear from the ground and collect into the sacks on the back of the machine Mr. Verity and the spectators gave a loud cheer. The rousing shouts were heard by their neighbours in Manor Farm.

News reached Manor Farm that the potato picker had been delivered and implemented on-site. It was a great success. The potato picker developed and built by the pigs had been locked away in a shed, never to be seen or referred to again. Hearing the news that Mr. Verity had built a successful machine, Franco decided that their potato picker would be taken out of storage and used once more. Alfred, the pig charged with building the machine made a few modifications to enable it to work more successfully. The potato picker did help the harvesting each autumn, although not as successful as it could have been. It was also part of the centrepiece for the annual parades celebrating rebellion day and storm day. Each year the parades that had been led by the tractor were now led by the tractor and the potato picker as symbols of the advances in technology on Manor Farm.

Meanwhile, acting in co-operation, Pinchfield Farm and Beech Tree Farm shared the potato picker developed by Mr. Verity to make their autumn harvest very simple and straightforward. Using the expertise acquired to develop this first piece of technology, they made further advances in farm machinery. They developed a seed driller that enabled them to plant endless rows of seeds effortlessly. They also developed a muck spreader that could be attached to the back of their tractor which helped to enrich the soil and produce higher yields of their crops. Then they produced a cutting machine for the annual corn harvest. As the years went by, they created a whole collection of farm machinery that made life easier and also improved productivity and yields. Franco was aware of these developments and did his best to play down their impact. Trumpet continued to proclaim that Manor Farm was a leading farm in machinery and developments on other farms were much exaggerated.

Chapter VI

Whilst Trumpet continued to proclaim that Manor Farm was developing suitable farm machinery and other farms exaggerated their progress, Franco knew that Beech Tree Farm, in conjunction with Pinchfield Farm, was making great strides in mechanisation. Franco was jealous and annoyed by this development. He decided that something would need to be done to improve their relative position. The patrols along the boundary between the two halves of Pinchfield Farm were told that they should pay special attention to any activity on the side belonging to Mr. Lawrence, with particular attention to any farm machinery. They were told to get as many details as they could about the nature of the equipment, its purpose and the way it was built. This carried on for some weeks, but it soon became obvious to Franco that their long-range surveillance was not adequate to get the information that he required.

Franco decided that they would have to introduce a much more daring plan. They would have to go on to Pinchfield Farm and inspect the farm machinery close-up. When he told his idea to the rest of the pigs they were alarmed. They thought that the chances of getting away with this intrusion were slim. None of them volunteered to cross the fence and enter into the neighbouring farm. Also it was felt that it would be too obvious if one of the pigs were seen wandering around Pinchfield. Of course, following the transformation which had taken effect a long time ago, it was almost impossible to distinguish the pigs from human beings. However, the pigs were still concerned and would not volunteer for the task.

After much discussion, they agreed that one of the farmhands sympathetic to their cause would be chosen to creep surreptitiously through a gap in the fence, have a look in the farm buildings at the machinery and report back. The person chosen was a young, agile farmhand called Nicholas Handy. On the first evening he met with Franco and two more pigs to discuss the task they had selected for him to undertake. Being one of the few humans loyal to the pigs, Nick, as he was known, agreed to undertake the task.

Armed with only a torch, Nick proceeded to go through the gate, which separated Manor Farm from Pinchfield Farm and then onto the fence which separated the two halves of Pinchfield farm. Whilst there were regular patrols along the Manor Farm side of the fence, there were only occasional patrols along the Beech Tree Farm side. These could hardly be called patrols because they consisted of a member of Mr. Verity's staff walking along the fence to make sure that all was in order. Nick had no trouble climbing over the fence and entering into Pinchfield Farm. He half expected the sound of barking dogs, which is what he would have found if he climbed over the wrong way. However, Mr. Lawrence's half of Pinchfield Farm was quiet and undisturbed. It was a full moon that evening and Nick could make his way to the farm buildings with little trouble. Once he arrived at the buildings he peered through the windows to check that there was nobody about. Reassuring himself that he was alone, he ventured to open one of the doors to look inside. Trusting that there would be no intruders, Mr. Verity did not bother to lock the doors of the outbuildings. Once inside, Nick could see that the building housed an advanced type of plough and a seed driller. He realised that he should have brought some means of taking notes, but it was too late. He decided that he had done enough this evening and would return the next night with pencil and paper to make drawings and detailed notes.

The following day was overcast and cloudy. It made it more difficult to climb the fence and cross the field to get to the farm building. Nick managed to get through and once more entered the building containing the plough and the seed driller. Using his torch he could see clearly enough to make drawings and notes. Each item was meticulously drawn and labelled but this was a lengthy process. As he worked, the farm building creaked and groaned in the wind. Nick thought that he could hear someone approaching the building but no-one arrived. After two hours, he thought he could not risk staying any longer. He collected up his papers, pencil, and torch and made his way back to Manor Farm. Franco was very pleased with his efforts. He could see that he could make use of the drawings to develop machinery for Manor Farm. It was agreed that Nick would return one more time to see what other information he could get.

Unfortunately, he dropped a piece of blank paper. It was found by one of the farmhands and given to Mr. Verity. The blank piece of paper in itself was not incriminating. However, Mr. Verity's suspicions were aroused. He thought it would do no harm to keep watch on the farm buildings that evening. If there had been an intruder, then if they returned they would be caught; if there were no intruder, all they would do is lose a few hours' sleep.

The following night, Nick set off once more. He made his way through the gate into Pinchfield Farm, crossed over to the fence, climbed over and moved stealthily to the outbuildings. He made his way carefully around the building that he had entered before and approached a second building that looked large enough to contain farm machinery. As he put his hand on the door knob two large muscular farmhands appeared, one on each side. Each farmhand took an arm and escorted him unceremoniously to a farm building. Once inside, he was confronted by Mr. Verity. Nicholas Handy was interrogated by Mr. Verity and the farmhands and even threatened with physical violence. He refused to say what he was doing on the farm. Finally, they gave up the interrogation and locked him up in a small outbuilding, providing him with blankets and food. Nick jumped each time he heard footsteps. He was expecting his captors to threaten him again. He knew that if the situation was reversed, Franco would not hesitate; he would set the dogs on the prisoner. However, Nick was left alone except when meals were delivered. It seemed he would remain there for the rest of his life.

Mr. Verity was troubled by this intrusion. It seemed obvious that behind this escapade was Franco of Manor Farm. Mr. Verity decided that he would increase the patrols along the fence and he would ask his men to pay particular attention to any activity on the other side. He warned them that they should not instigate any trouble and they should keep on their side of the fence to avoid being attacked by the dogs. The farmhands increased their patrols for several days but, like Franco, Mr. Verity realised that there was very little chance of collecting information from this far away. Manor

Farm house was the centre of activity for Franco and the other pigs and it could not be seen from Pinchfield Farm. However it could be seen from certain points around Manor Farm. Mr. Verity decided that the farmhands would have to be more audacious and start moving around the perimeter of Manor Farm to see what Franco and the others were doing.

One of the farmhands, Andrew Newton, was given a pair of powerful binoculars and told to go all the way around the outside of Manor Farm as far as he could to see what, if anything was going on. This was early summer; the days were longer so that Andy could make use of the evening light and his binoculars to survey Manor Farm. After his first evening's expedition, he reported back to Mr. Verity that there was very little to be seen other than the usual activities one would expect around the farm. However, he would try once more to see if anything else was happening.

The following evening, Andy Newton went off once more to survey Manor Farm walking around the perimeter of the farm. He looked for suitable spots that would give him a clear sight of the activities on the farm. Although he tried as best he could to gain an advantage point, he realised that there was little opportunity to see very much from such a distance. At the northern end of the farm was a wood. Andy realised that if he gained entry into the wood then he could approach the farmhouse and get a good view of what was happening. Whilst he considered this was perhaps a risky business, he thought that the pigs would be too absorbed in what they were doing and not be thinking about any activity in the neglected wood. He climbed over the fence which circled the whole boundary of Manor Farm and proceeded as carefully and as quietly as he could into the wood and through to the side closest to the farmhouse. As he approached the edge of the wood, careful not to reveal himself, he raised his binoculars and surveyed the scene in front of him.

Unfortunately, whilst concentrating on the farmhouse he had not noticed the dogs bounding towards him. When they got close they started barking and intimidating him. He felt for certain that the dogs would harm or even kill him. As these dreadful thoughts went through his mind, one of the pigs arrived and told the dogs to heel. Andy Newton had little choice but to go with the pig and the dogs to the farmhouse. Inside the farmhouse he was confronted by Franco and the other pigs. He blustered that this was all a mistake. He was out bird watching and had inadvertently strayed into the wood. He was very sorry it would not happen again and, please, could he go home. Franco and the pigs were having none of this. They confiscated his binoculars, locked him in an outbuilding, and informed Mr. Verity that one of his staff had been caught in the grounds of Manor Farm.

Franco and the pigs continued to question Andy Newton, threatening him, his family and his friends. Eventually Harry confessed that he was spying on the farmhouse on the instructions of Mr. Verity. Trumpet made sure that everybody in the area knew that Andy Newton had been apprehended, that Mr. Verity was spying on other farms, and Manor Farm was well within its rights to imprison the spy for as long as they felt was necessary.

A meeting was quietly arranged between a representative of Manor Farm and a representative of Pinchfield Farm to be held in the office of Mr. Whymper. Both sides understood that the other was holding one of their farmhands. At first there was table thumping and protestations that the other side had acted unethically, unfairly and illegally. However, it became apparent that both sides were actually in a similar position. It was agreed that the two farmhands Andy Newton and Nicholas Handy would be exchanged. This would be facilitated by an independent person from Mr. Whymper's office. So the following morning, Franco and the pigs led Andy Newton to the fence separating the two halves of Pinchfield. From the other direction came Mr. Verity, with two of his farmhands accompanying Nicholas Handy. When both parties had reached the fence, Mr. Arbuthnot from Mr. Whymper's office supervised the exchange of the two people. He looked on whilst simultaneously the two climbed over the dividing fence reaching their own half once more. Abruptly Franco and his entourage turned round and marched back to the farmhouse. In the same way, Mr. Verity and his party turned and went back to the farm buildings.

Both Andy Newton and Nick Handy were treated as heroes by their friends and colleagues when they returned to their respective farms.

Chapter VII

The incident involving Andy Newton and Nick Handy did nothing to help the situation between Beech Tree Farm and Manor Farm. Both sides were apprehensive about the other. Over the coming months, the level of tension grew between the two farms. Mr. Verity was well aware of the boundary between the two halves of Pinchfield Farm and that Franco was keen to keep them separated. However, the construction overnight of an enormous barbed wire fence surprised even Mr. Verity.

During the night, a group of labourers from the village employed by Mr. Arbuthnot on the instructions of Franco had arrived at Manor Farm. They were accompanied by several trucks carrying rolls of barbed wire. Using generators and arc lamps the men worked through the night supervised by Trumpet. The farm was surrounded by a high fence. This was topped by barbed wire ensuring that no animal or person could cross from one side to the other in either direction. The men worked stealthily and undetected through the night. They finished just before dawn. Once finished, they cleared their tools, the generators and arc lamps, leaving no trace that they had been there.

On the Manor Farm side of the fence the dogs patrolled the complete length of the new barbed wire fence. Day and night the patrols kept watch. Any person or animal straying near the fence knew they would receive swift retribution from the dogs. On the other side of the fence, Mr. Verity kept an eye on what was happening. Occasionally, a member of staff would walk along the fence to make sure that nothing untoward was happening on the other side.

Some years before, Mr. Frederick had invaded Manor Farm with a group of his workers. They had attempted to take over the farm and in the process had demolished the windmill using dynamite. Franco had not forgotten this. Since the invasion, he had been secretly purchasing and storing dynamite that he thought he could make use of one day. He had reluctantly split Pinchfield Farm down the middle giving responsibility for one half to the owners of Beech Tree Farm. Franco longed for the day when he could take over complete ownership of Pinchfield and possibly even Beech Tree Farm. To this end he amassed the dynamite

Over the months Mr. Verity was informed that there was increased activity along the fence. There were more dogs patrolling. He increased the patrols along his side of the fence to keep an eye on what Franco was doing. The patrols started carrying shotguns as a way of showing that they meant business. In response the dogs increased their patrol of the boundary. They were joined by a pig carrying the old shotgun that had been owned by Mr. Jones.

For several months, the two farms confronted each other across the barbed wire. Meanwhile the pigs opened up an unused shed near the separating fence. The pigs were seen to be carrying boxes into the shed, stockpiling whatever they contained. Listening to the gossip about Manor Farm, Mr. Verity came to realise that the pigs were stockpiling dynamite in the shed near the fence.

Mr. Verity sent a message to Franco telling him that he should remove the dynamite and reduce the patrol along the fence. Franco refused and instead increased the patrols along the fence in expectation of an anticipated invasion. Mr. Verity repeated his request to Franco. Again he refused. Beech Tree Farm and Pinchfield Farm enlisted the aid of the surrounding farms. Representatives from the farms met with the local stores who agreed that they would not trade with Manor Farm. They refused to sell goods to Manor Farm or buy its produce whilst Franco continued his stance against Pinchfield Farm. Of course, Franco was furious. He could be heard in the farmhouse at all hours shouting at anyone within range:

"How dare they tell me what to do on my farm! What right have they to stop me stockpiling anything I want in my shed! I will deal with them!"

He refused to remove the dynamite or reduce the patrols along the barbed wire between the two halves of Pinchfield Farm.

Mr. Verity continued to demand the withdrawal. Local buyers and sellers continued to their embargo on Manor Farm. After a while this embargo started to have some impact on the lives of the animals on Manor Farm. Not being able to sell produce meant that they were not receiving the hard cash that they needed for purchasing essential supplies. In any case it would be impossible to buy these supplies, for example, supplementary feed, because of the embargo on selling to Manor Farm. The animals became disgruntled. The pigs started to miss what they considered to be their essentials, including their beer. The pressure mounted on Franco to withdraw from the border but he refused to do so. The embargo helped focus attention on the problem of stockpiling dynamite, but was not entirely successful in making Franco remove the dynamite stockpile which was held in the shed.

Meanwhile Mr. Verity, threatened by the build up of dogs, guns and dynamite, was beginning to feel frustrated and annoyed. He decided to put on a show of force along the boundary wire. He asked several of the farmers and farm hands in the neighbourhood to join him early one morning. They started marching toward the barbed wire each carrying a gun. One of the dogs on patrol immediately ran to the farmhouse and informed the pigs that the delegation could be seen moving towards the barbed wire. One of the pigs nervously informed Franco of the position. He immediately got very cross and marched toward the barbed wire, followed by a contingent of pigs and dogs. When they were confronting each other across the wire, Mr. Verity said in a loud, firm voice. "I will not tolerate this build-up of dynamite close to the border between the two halves of the farm. This is threatening behaviour and is not acceptable." Franco replied "This is our farm and we can do what we like to protect our interests." Mr. Verity responded by saying "This is not acceptable. You are responsible for Manor Farm but you are looking after Pinchfield Farm only until it is returned to its rightful owners. You have no mandate to stockpile dynamite on this land. You will stop; if you refuse to do so we will take up arms against you."

Mr. Verity and Franco faced each other in a seemingly impossible stand-off. The other humans and animals became very nervous. It looked like there was going to be an all-out war between the two sides. Mr. Verity and Franco faced each other for what seemed like an interminable amount of time. Mr. Verity stood fast not budging or blinking. Franco on the other hand, started to look more nervous, shifting from trotter to trotter. He knew that Mr. Verity had more weapons and more people. Whilst Manor Farm could become involved in conflict, the outcome was uncertain at best, total annihilation at worst. Franco decided reluctantly to arrange a negotiation.

Further along the fence away from the stand-off between Mr. Verity and Franco a meeting took place. The meeting involved Mr. Verity's brother Percival and Columbus a pig trusted by Franco. They started by restating the arguments that had been presented before. Percival Verity said that Beech Tree Farm could not allow the build-up of dynamite so close to their farms. Columbus replied that they would do whatever they wanted to on their side of the fence. Initially it seemed that this meeting was going to end in deadlock. However, Percival Verity suggested that they could reach some agreement that would satisfy both sides and neither side would lose face. He insisted that Manor Farm should remove the dynamite from their side of the fence. In return, Beech Tree Farm and Pinchfield Farm would not show any form of aggression on their side of the fence. Percival Verity promised on behalf of his brother and the farms that they would never undertake any act of hostility against Manor Farm. Columbus trusted Percival Verity and agreed to stand down. Percival Verity and Columbus shook hand and trotter on the deal. They both returned to their groups on either side of the fence. Both Franco and Mr. Verity recognised that this was a reasonable agreement which averted the possibility of a disastrous conflict between the two sides.

Franco ordered that the dynamite should be removed from the shed and transported back to Manor Farm, where it was safely stored away. The dogs continued to patrol the barbed wire but their numbers reduced. On the other side of the fence, Mr. Verity's staff continued to walk occasionally along the length of the wire to ensure that there were no signs of active aggression on the other side. The local stores opened their doors to Manor Farm once more so that they could buy and sell their goods, produce and provisions.

Trumpet collected together the animals of Manor Farm. He announced that Franco and the farm had achieved a great victory. Despite the overwhelming numbers and weapons of Beech Tree Farm, Franco had stood up to Mr. Verity and his friends and showed them that they would not tolerate interference. Because of Franco's supreme effort the local stores had been forced into buying and selling with them once more.

All humans and most animals thought that the outcome was reasonable. Catastrophe had been avoided and there was an uneasy peace between Manor Farm and the other farms in the area. However, some of the pigs were unhappy. They thought that Franco was too soft. Rather than negotiate a deal through Columbus, he should have stood up to Mr. Verity whatever the outcome. These pigs wanted a return to the hard line of Napoleon. They considered that Manor Farm should achieve a prominence in the area by force if necessary. The discontented pigs did nothing for the time being; they continued to plot amongst themselves whilst biding their time.

The immediate danger of full-scale conflict between Beech Tree Farm and Manor Farm had passed but there continued to be a tension between the two farms. Neither side trusted the other. Franco continued to believe that he should have the whole of Pinchfield Farm, giving him an opportunity to take over Beech Tree Farm as well. On the other hand Mr. Verity believed that Franco and Manor Farm continued to be a threat which would be much reduced if Franco and the pigs were no longer running the farm. As the seasons changed from summer to autumn to winter the relations between Manor Farm and Beech Tree Farm became frostier.

Neither side trusted the other. Whilst there was no build-up of dynamite or other evidence of aggression along the fence separating the two sides, both sides continued to maintain a supply of guns and dynamite in case they were needed if they were attacked. Outwardly there was some communication between Franco and Mr. Verity. It would appear that whilst they were not the best of friends, they were at least talking to each other. However, behind this facade of communication, there was a sense of mistrust and uncertainty. This state of tension was to continue for several years.

Chapter VIII

Over the years, Beech Tree Farm grew into a successful enterprise. Mr. Verity was regarded as a good farmer. He was firm but fair with his workers. The welfare of the animals was uppermost in his thoughts. He treated them all with dignity and respect. His reputation was widely known. His customers knew that he would charge fair prices, sell only good produce, and deliver on time. Consequently he was known for good customer service.

Not all Mr. Verity's customers dealt personally with him. Some of the larger customers would go through a process of putting out contracts to tender. Mr. Verity would read through the contract, see if Beech Tree Farm could supply the necessary goods and then submit a tender giving his prices and delivery schedule. This system had worked well in the past. Big customers would have a list of favoured supplies and, of course, because of his reputation, Mr. Verity would be on the list. Over the years he had won his fair share of such contracts.

A similar process to selling was part of the buying process for the farm. Most items could be purchased through various suppliers across the counter. Such items were subject to a clearly stated price list albeit with discount for large quantities and prompt payment. The suppliers were well aware of Mr. Verity's reputation. This enabled him to negotiate good discounts because the suppliers knew they would be paid promptly and in full. In addition to across the counter buying there were occasional auctions. These could be for livestock, machinery, vehicles, and other large items. Traditionally, such auctions had been verbal, noisy affairs. An auctioneer would manage the proceedings and all interested buyers would gather round the item for sale and signal when they wanted to bid. Whilst this was still the case for the farmers' auction in town, other auctions allowed telephone or postal sealed bids. Mr. Verity, like other busy farmers, did not want to lose a day's work on the farm by attending an auction for one item. Knowing the values of items he would often enter a sealed bid for such items. Again over the years he had won his fair share of auction lots.

Mr. Verity had maintained Beech Tree Farm as a profitable venture by being reasonable with his tenders for customers and his bids for auction lots. The machinery and vehicles he had bought had enabled him to successfully mechanise the farm to the point where it was becoming very efficient. However, over the last few months Mr. Verity had been less successful in his business dealings. He felt that he was not winning contracts as often as he had in the past. Also he was not winning lots at auction. He decided to pay more attention to his tenders, bids and their outcomes.

Checking his transactions Mr. Verity noted that he was missing out on business deals. Whilst the outcomes of tenders and contracts were not made public, the good relationship which Mr. Verity enjoyed with his customers and suppliers meant that he could ask them informally why he was not winning any more. He was shocked but not surprised by their replies. They reported that Beech Tree Farm was missing out on tender contracts by very small amounts of money. Generally the successful tenders were from Manor or Foxwood Farm. The same was true for auction bids. Several items that Mr. Verity bid for had been won by a small margin by Manor or Foxwood Farm. He decided to investigate further.

Mr. Verity knew that he could not approach his customers directly and ask them to share confidential information. However he did want to find out why his tenders were being beaten on a regular basis and by such small margins. He enlisted the aid of an old and trusted customer with whom he had worked for several years. Mr. Bartholomew was currently asking for tenders for the supply of potatoes for his farm shops. Mr. Verity sat down and worked out what was a reasonable price for the quantity required and a delivery schedule he thought would be reasonably easy to match up to. Once the tender was completed, he sealed the envelope and gave it to Ted James, a trusted farmhand, to post the following day. The next day as requested Ted went into Willingdon, the local town, and posted the tender.

The day after the tender was posted; Verity visited Mr. Bartholomew, knowing that the letter would be delivered that day. Both men looked very carefully at the post especially the letter they knew had come contained the tender. It was clear by looking at the envelope that it had been tampered with. It had been opened and resealed. Anybody opening the envelope without any degree of suspicion would not have noticed the tampering but both Mr. Verity and Mr. Bartholomew were looking particularly for any sign of interference. Mr. Bartholomew opened the envelope and read the tender. Mr. Verity agreed that the contents had not been altered in any way. The price and delivery dates were as he had written them two days ago. It would have been unethical for Mr. Bartholomew to show the other tenders from the rivals of Mr. Verity. He agreed to open the tenders privately. Looking through the tenders, he found that the lowest tender was indeed from Manor Farm. He would not reveal the actual amounts but he did state that the difference was small but enough to deny Beech Tree Farm the tender. Mr. Verity thanked Mr. Bartholomew and went back to Beech Tree wondering what to do next.

Mr. Verity knew that something had happened to the tender between his writing it on the Monday and its being delivered on the Wednesday. He could not believe that Ted James could be involved in anything underhand but he decided to submit another tender and see what happens. A few weeks later, Mr. Bartholomew informed the local farmers that he required another schedule of potatoes because his shops were doing good business. This gave Mr. Verity the opportunity to observe Ted's behaviour once more. He worked out a price and a delivery rota. He included these in a tender which he then sealed in an envelope ready for posting by Ted James the following morning. However, Mr. Verity also completed a second tender based on a slightly lower but fair price and a reasonable delivery rota. This tender he placed in another envelope ready to be posted. The following morning, Mr. Verity told Ted James that he had to go into town to buy provisions. Whilst he was in Willingdon he could post the letter which Ted James was holding onto. Reluctantly Ted handed over the letter. Verity noticed that the envelope showed small but clear signs of tampering. He pocketed the envelope and posted the true tender with the lower price. Two days later he was informed by Mr. Bartholomew that his tender had been successful and had undercut any other tender by a small but significant amount. Mr. Bartholomew confirmed that the next lowest tender was indeed from Manor Farm.

Mr. Verity was now convinced that the tampering was taking place on Pinchfield before the letter was taken to the post office. This meant that Ted James was somehow involved in the conspiracy to ensure that Manor Farm was successful in its underhand attempts to win tenders. Mr. Verity called Ted into his office in the farmhouse and asked him directly what was going on. Ted denied all knowledge of any wrongdoing. He said that when he was given the envelope he took it back to the farm hands' cottage and put it on the mantelpiece where it was safe until the following morning. At which time he would take the envelope into town and post it. He had never seen anybody in the cottage, near the cottage or tampering with the envelope. For the moment, Mr. Verity let it go at that. But he was convinced something sinister was happening. Meanwhile, on Manor Farm, Franco was concerned that he had lost the latest tender to Mr. Bartholomew. Knowing everything about Mr. Verity's tenders and bids gave him a definite but dishonest advantage.

On Beech Tree Farm there was a small herd of distinctive Oxford Sandy and Black pigs all from the same litter. Their breed was named after their distinctive sandy and black blotchy coats. Mr. Verity had bought them two years before at a local farm market. He was never entirely happy with this group of pigs and felt they could not be trusted. They seemed to be particularly nosy rooting around the farmhouse and listening in on conversations. Two of the Oxford pigs, Tom and Dick were warned by a third Oxford pig, Harry, that Mr. Verity had his suspicions about their behaviour. Mr. Verity believed they were tampering with tenders. That night, under cover of darkness, Tom and Dick both fled to Manor Farm.

Following their sudden departure, Mr. Verity was once more successful in his tenders and bids. He won his fair share which was no more or less than he expected. Meanwhile, he wondered if any other animals, pigs in particular, were in league with Franco and Manor Farm. He continued to be fair with all the animals but he kept a watchful eye on them all. Harry, the third Oxford pig, became more and more nervous that he was under suspicion. A few weeks later, he too fled to Manor Farm. He was expecting a hero's welcome having been passing on information about Beech Tree Farm for years. However, Franco did not trust Harry. If he could spy for him then he could spy for Mr. Verity. Harry lived not as a hero in the farmhouse but isolated in an old shed with meagre rations. Eventually Harry was accepted into the farmhouse and feed well on bran, milk and beer. When he died he was given a big burial organised by Franco.

After the departure of the three pigs, Verity believed that there were at least two others. Sometime later Jack confessed to being the fourth pig but denied that there was ever a fifth pig. Jack gave Mr. Verity the whole history of the pigs' links to Manor Farm. He explained how Franco could get the information about tenders and bids. Ted James, the farmhand, had a gambling problem and the pigs used this to bribe him to intercept letters on their way to the post office. Subsequently Ted had fallen ill, retired and gone to live with his sister in Shropshire.

A couple of years later, Mr. Verity retired still believing that there was a fifth pig but he never did find out which one it was. He was fairly certain that it was another Oxford Sandy and Black but he went to live in a bungalow on the coast not knowing. The farm was bought by Mr. Wordsworth. Like Mr. Verity, he ran Beech Tree Farm honestly and fairly.

Chapter IX

Franco continued to lead Manor Farm; however, some of the pigs thought that he was losing touch. He had denounced Napoleon on several occasions and his policy of moving away from confrontation with the other farms was seen as destructive and destabilising. They felt that Franco had failed in several recent events. He had exchanged spies, backed down when confronted about the dynamite and barbed wire fencing, and he had been embarrassed by the scandal of the five pigs, most of who had come to live on Manor farm. As Franco grew older, his erratic behaviour became worse. The group of pigs felt that he was making decisions without discussing or confirming them with the rest of the pigs. One day he was visiting Foxwood Farm. Whilst he was away the group of pigs decided to get together and force an end to the problem. When Franco returned, he was forced to resign. He was immediately replaced by Ethelred an old Large White pig. The group felt that Ethelred would return to a more traditional style of leadership. Trumpet the spokespig for Franco was also forced to resign and was replaced by Clarion, a pig that would support the group and Ethelred.

As the months passed, Pinchfield Farm and Beech Tree farm continued to enjoy the success of their mechanisation. It became evident to surrounding farms that both were thriving, successful and happy places to work. Meanwhile, Manor Farm was becoming more and more isolated. Clarion the spokespig for Manor Farm continued to give out messages that it was doing well. Production was increasing year on year. All the animals were very happy working on the farm and contented. Mr. Arbuthnot, one of the few humans to visit the farm, also carried the message that Manor Farm was doing well. However, this was based on the verbal encouragement from Clarion and little factual evidence. Manor Farm, along with Foxwood Farm, remained a mystery to the surrounding farms.

Ethelred, the leading pig of Manor Farm, decided that the farm should have its place in society and history. He called all the pigs and the Pilkingtons together to discuss how they could improve the image of Manor Farm. After much discussion, they agreed that something ought to be done. One way of improving the image of Manor and Foxwood Farms would be to become involved in the agricultural exhibitions that were run throughout the county and beyond. Several categories were considered but neither farm had the necessary animals or skills to compete in most of them. They decided that they would enter their prized cows into the exhibitions. The day arrived and Michael Pilkington transported the cows to an exhibition not far from Manor Farm. It soon became evident that the cows being exhibited were nowhere near as fine as the cows that were there from other farms that were well fed, well treated and looked in fine condition. Inevitably the cows exhibited by Michael Pilkington did not win any prizes.

Michael Pilkington went back to Manor Farm and entered into deep discussion with Ethelred. They realised that it would be difficult winning any prize based on livestock. They considered exhibiting crops such as potatoes but again realised that they had little chance of winning any prizes. In the end, Michael Pilkington and Ethelred decided that they would enter a prestigious event – the sheep dog trials. The dogs on Manor Farm were bred specifically to maintain order for the pigs. However, their heritage was as sheepdogs. Consequently they chose three of the friendliest looking dogs to be the competitors in the future sheepdog trials. Michael Pilkington agreed to be the sheep dog handler who would represent Manor and Foxwood Farms. The sheep on Manor Farm had always been compliant. They had followed the instructions of Napoleon and Franco and, nowadays, they followed Ethelred. They were known to chant the appropriate song of the time. The combination of Michael Pilkington, the three dogs and the benign sheep, they were sure, could be used effectively to make a significant entry into sheepdog trials.

Sheepdog trials consisted of a farmer and his dogs managing a herd of sheep. They had to be rounded up, driven through a pair of gates, circled around a pen, and, then, be driven into the pen. The gate would be closed and the trial finished. Marks were awarded for the way in which the sheep kept together, the speed with which the farmer could complete the task and the satisfactory completion of the tasks. Michael Pilkington started working with the dogs to teach them to follow orders when handling the sheep. It soon became apparent that the dogs that had been the enforcers for Franco were not necessarily well suited to the task of gently guiding the sheep. However, with some practice the dogs started to obey orders and gave the impression of being well-practised sheep dogs. The sheep not being used to such rigorous control took some time to get used to the idea that they were going to be herded and directed into the necessary locations in the field.

After three months of training, Mr. Pilkington entered the dogs and the sheep into the first trial at an animal fair not far from the farm. Using his old Land Rover and trailer he transported both sheep and dogs to the location. Other farmers from around the county were surprised to see that Foxwood Farm had entered into the competition.

When it was the turn of Mr. Pilkington to compete, the dogs listened to the commands made by whistles from Mr. Pilkington and directed the sheep. Accordingly, the trial went well enough, but was not perfect. One or two sheep were always wandering off in the wrong direction. The dogs tried hard to work with Mr. Pilkington and not take it upon themselves to manage the sheep. It took a great deal of restraint by the dogs not to grab the sheep by the throat and drag them around the field to the defined finishing point. Twelve teams entered the sheepdog trials. Mr. Pilkington came eleventh beating one farmer who was completely hopeless.

Back at Manor Farm, Mr. Pilkington met with Ethelred to discuss the outcome of the sheep dog trial. Whilst it was not a complete disaster, Ethelred was disappointed that the farmer and dogs had not put up a much better show for the rest of the farming community. Ethelred decided that they needed to act. The dogs whilst appearing to be normal sheepdogs being firm but friendly became more vicious in their control of the sheep. In turn, the sheep were warned that if they did not improve their performance they would be destroyed by the dogs. The sheep were being coerced by Mr. Pilkington and tormented by the dogs. Nonetheless, they were being treated as celebrities on the farm. They were kept together in a field and housed in a shed isolated from not only the other sheep but all animals on the farm. Whilst this appeared to be favouritism by the rest of the animals, the reality was that the sheep were living in miserable conditions. Each day they had to work hard and practise for eight hours a day. They were fed very little so that they would keep their weight down, enabling them to be more agile around the field.

Following a couple of months of this regime, they entered another competition. This time the sheep behaved almost impeccably under the threat of savagery from the dogs. All the tasks were completed and the judges gave good marks for the dogs and sheep apparently working together in harmony. Overall they achieved sixth position in a field of twelve teams. Where they failed was in the timing of the exercise, the sheep were slow both in terms of thought and action. Once more Pilkington met with Ethelred to discuss what needed to be done to improve the position of the Foxwood Farm team. They agreed that little could be done to improve the thought processes of the sheep who generally were the slowest thinkers on the farm. This was true, not just for their team, but all the teams that entered into competitions. What they could think about was how to improve the speed of the sheep around the field. They were already on a restricted diet so that they were not carrying as much weight as other sheep at the trials. However,

Ethelred believed they could move faster. He decided to supplement their diet with steroids that would help build their muscles and make them move faster.

Two months later, they entered another competition. This time the sheep were good at following commands coerced by the threat of the dogs. They were also much better at getting around the field because of their increased muscle. Consequently, they finished third in the field of twelve entrants. Pilkington and Ethelred were pleased with this improvement and they continued with the regime. The sheep remained in isolation following the strict diet, including the steroids, prescribed by Ethelred. Of course, the sheep were unaware that they were being manipulated by drugs. The dogs continued to threaten them should they fail in practice or in the actual event.

The next event came along and Pilkington with the dogs and sheep entered. This time, much to the delight of Pilkington and Ethelred, the team came first. Other farms were surprised but impressed that the Pilkington team had reached such a standard in such a short time. Ethelred believed that Manor Farm through the involvement of Mr. Pilkington and Foxwood farm was achieving its rightful place in the eyes of the surrounding farms. The sheepdog trials showed the world how successful Ethelred and Manor Farm could be.

This success carried on for several sheepdog trials at county fairs and farm shows. However there was an unfortunate side-effect of the sheep's regime. As they gained muscle, enormous stress was placed on their hearts and circulatory systems. One by one the sheep started to suffer health problems. Rather than getting quicker they slowed down, finding it difficult to breath and walk any distance at all. One by one, the sheep started to die. These were replaced by other sheep that were selected from the rest of the herd on the farm on Manor Farm.

It became evident to other entrants in the sheepdog trials that the Foxwood herd of sheep was changing fairly frequently during the sheep dog trials. Whilst sheep have a relatively short life, they could still participate in the trials for several years. Most people could not tell one sheep from another but the farmers involved in the sheepdog trials, of course, were skilled in working with sheep. They could easily identify their individual sheep and the individual sheep of their rivals. As their anxieties grew, the other farmers asked the governing body of sheepdog trials to investigate their concerns.

The governing body decided that to ensure fairness farmers would no longer use their own sheep in the sheepdog trials. A large herd of sheep was bred purposefully to provide the sheep for the trials. At each sheepdog trial a small herd would be randomly selected from the whole herd for each farmer to use in their part of the competition. This proved a temporary problem for most farmers who in the past knew their sheep individually and could rely upon them to perform. It was a disaster for Mr. Pilkington. His dogs, that in the past had used threats and coercion to make sure that their sheep followed instructions, could no longer rely on this approach under the watchful eye of the judges. Their apparent firm and friendly approach did not work well when trying to drive the sheep around the field, through the gates and into the pen. It soon became obvious that Mr. Pilkington and his dogs would not be winning any more competitions.

Ethelred decided that Manor Farm would withdraw from public competitions. The dogs returned to their task of keeping order on Manor Farm. The surviving sheep that had lived through a regime of endless practice and steroids did not live for much longer.

Although the sheep dog trials were less than successful, Ethelred wanted to maintain a presence in the activities of farms in the neighbourhood. Every two years there was a gala organised by one particular farm. Whilst this should have a friendly gathering, the galas were often marred by inter-farm rivalry and lack of goodwill.

The following year the gala was hosted by Maple Farm. It was a jolly day. There were exhibitions of various farm activities, races for humans and animals, and a dinner in the evening attended by all. Everything would have been well but a lot of the farms south of Maple Farm boycotted the gala. They complained that Maple Farm had invited New Farm, a large sheep farm. New Farm had cooperated with South Farm who had upset the other farms because of their treatment of animals. Despite the boycott, the gala was successful. Following the example of Maple Farm, Ethelred decided that hosting the Gala would be good for the publicity of Manor Farm.

The other farms agreed and Ethelred and the other pigs started to make plans. They had two years to create a gala arena and suitable accommodation for the visits. To do this, energy and resources were diverted from the farm labours to the gala. The animals had to work longer hours for less rations but they were told that the gala would open up the farm and be a long term benefit. Eventually the preparations were complete and Manor Farm was ready for the gala. As the day approached, Pinchfield Farm, Beech Tree Farm, and several other farms announced that they would not attend the gala as a protest against Manor Farm's retaining interest in Foxwoods and Pinchfield Farms. On the day only half the usual number of farms attended. Guests arrived at the gates and after some scrutiny they were escorted to the area designated for the gala. Pigs and dogs kept in the background but it was clear that they were patrolling the areas that were not to be accessed by visitors. Despite the restrictions, the gala was a reasonable success. The pigs and lower animals were ordered to behave loyally in front of the guests. Exhibitions were given, races were run and the gala concluded with a triumphal dinner in the barn. To the outside world, Manor Farm had done well to organise the gala which was regarded as a success. The animals knew how much the gala had cost in terms of hard work and suffering.

Two years later, the gala was organised by Beech Tree Farm providing a brand new enclosure and constructing a purpose-built building for the final dinner. In retaliation, Ethelred announced that Manor Farm would not attend the gala. Nonetheless, the event was held and it was considered to be a great success. However, once more the gala did not have a full complement of farms which contradicted the idea that the gala would bring farms together to meet and compete peacefully.

The following gala held in Lone Tree Farm was completely free from boycotts, the first for many years. The gala went well but future galas were inevitably open to rivalries and politics. The other farms remembered the sheep dog trials and there were lingering suspicions that any involvement from Manor Farm was not always above board.

Chapter X

For many years, Ethelred ruled Manor Farm and indirectly Foxwood Farm and half of Pinchfield Farm as well. Over time, he grew older and more and more infirm. He desperately hung onto power for as long as possible but eventually he became too ill and retired from everyday tasks. He was rarely seen around Manor Farm, other than exceptional days, for example, the anniversary of the triumph over Mr. Frederick and his invasion. One day, Ethelred was struck down by a severe bout of flu. Despite all the best efforts of the other pigs and visiting medics they could not save him. Soon after he died, Ethelred was given a large funeral with a procession to the orchard. He was buried alongside Napoleon and Franco. The pigs sang:

> Friend of fatherless!
> Fountain of happiness!
> Lord of the swill-bucket!
> Oh, how my soul is on
> Fire when I gaze at thy
> Calm and commanding eye,
> Like the sun in the sky,
> Comrade Ethelred!

The other pigs collected together to decide who would replace Ethelred. This was a more democratic process than had been the case in the past. Pigs were allowed to put names forward and support their particular choice. Finally, one pig called Victor was proposed by several of the other pigs and he was duly elected as the leader. Napoleon and Franco were both Berkshire boars and Ethelred was a Large White but Victor was a Tamworth with red-gold hair. He appeared softer and kinder than his predecessors.

Soon after his election, Victor announced a meeting of the animals. The following Sunday, they gathered in the barn to hear what their new leader had to say. Victor started by saying that they were going to enter into a new era. Over the past few years there had been a period of stagnation. They had been led by an old pig with little energy or enthusiasm for moving the farm forward. This was going to change. Victor announced that there would be more open leadership of the farm, any major decisions would involve all the animals, and any final decisions would be shared by all. No longer would there be one pig whose sole responsibility was to give information to the farm and the outside world. In the future information would be shared during meetings. The animals were pleased to hear that there were going to be changes in the future. However, they were concerned when they started to think about what Victor had told them. During his lifetime, they were told Ethelred was a good leader but now he was described as old and infirm. Some of the animals remembered that Napoleon and then Franco had been denigrated after their deaths.

They were not certain that Victor himself would continue to be held in high esteem. He talks about changes in the future but would these really happen? The animals could only wait to see what would happen in the future. It was not long before Victor had to tackle his first major problem.

The generator, bought and installed by Napoleon a long time ago, was barely adequate for the farm. It generated electricity which was used to light and heat the farmhouse and some heating and lighting in the other buildings. However it was large and unreliable. No animal on the farm including the pigs had any real idea about the workings of the generator. It was poorly maintained and never lubricated. It was topped up with diesel fuel when necessary and they believed that the generator would go on forever. The animals tolerated the presence of this machine because it did provide some warmth and light in the winter months. However there was always the noise and the smell of diesel.

One winter the generator was working particularly hard to keep up with the demand for electricity. It rattled and shook as its motor tried to turn the dynamo to create the heat and light.

However it could not keep up with the task in hand. The engine started to develop strange noises. There was a whirring noise from the bearings that had never been fully lubricated. There was a clanging from the depths of the engine as the parts rattled loose. And then it happened. There was a mighty explosion!

All the animals ran out into the yard to find out where the tremendous noise had come from. They rushed around the farmhouse to the side of the building where the generator was located. There they discovered that the generator was in a thousand pieces. Cogs, wheels, metal bars, and other parts were strewn around the farmyard. The explosion had completely destroyed the generator but even more alarmingly it had created a large hole in the side of the storage tank which had recently been filled with a delivery of diesel. The fuel was gushing out through the hole in the storage tank. A dank mixture of diesel and oil was flowing down the hill towards the stream at the bottom of the farm. This stream was important as it was a source of fresh water, not only for Manor Farm but also for Pinchfield Farm next door and Beech Tree Farm beyond that.

Manor Farm claimed it should have first calling on the water supply. This assertion had long been a cause of dispute between Manor Farm and the other farms. Some time ago Franco had threatened to cut off the water supply and force both Pinchfield and Beech Tree Farms to obtain water elsewhere. This would have involved considerable expense redirecting water around several miles to reach the farms. Mr. Wordsworth and Mr. Lawrence joined together to threaten Franco with retaliation if he did not maintain unrestricted access to the water supply for their farms. There was a period of intense confrontation. Eventually Franco realising the possible outcome gave way and allowed free and permanent unrestricted access to the water supply.

Now that supply was contaminated with oil and diesel, Mr. Wordsworth and Mr. Lawrence realised the implications immediately. They marched to the gate in the fence and told the pig patrolling on the other side that they wanted to see somebody in authority at once. When Victor arrived they demanded that he should allow them to assess the damage to the generator and try and sort out the contamination. Victor realising the seriousness of the situation agreed that they could enter the Manor Farm. Mr. Wordsworth and Mr. Lawrence were directed to the generator by an escort of pigs. The escort tried as much as possible to keep the two farmers from seeing anything else on Manor Farm. All the animals on the farm were given strict instructions not to talk to the two farmers or anybody else that would be involved with the generator.

Upon inspecting the generator, Mr. Wordsworth and Mr. Lawrence realised that little could be done to salvage it. There was little choice other than to shut it down completely. Mr. Wordsworth returned to his farm organised a gang of men and materials and returned to Manor farm to deal with the catastrophe. The farmhands mixed a batch of concrete and used it to create a barrier around the generator and blocked up all of the damage so that no more oil or diesel would be spilt. Then they looked at the stream which until the catastrophe had been pure, clear and fast-flowing. It now looked like sludge. Under the direction of the two farmers, the farmhands tried to skim off the oily foam that had collected on the surface of the stream, but the damage was too great. There was little that could be done to improve the quality of the stream in the short-term. All they could do was to make alternative arrangements until the stream had cleared itself. The only course of action was to transport water from upstream through to their farms until the stream was clear once more. The pollution had killed off local flora and fauna, flowers and fish. It was years before the river would completely restore itself and its wildlife.

Recognising the need to have a source of electricity, Victor organised a replacement generator to be bought and installed on the farm. This time several of the pigs were instructed in the use of the generator and how to maintain it so that it would prove trouble free during the following years. Of course, the new generator had to be paid for. Whilst it generated income from grinding corn for neighbouring farms, immediate payments were made by selling potatoes, grain and other supplies that had been stored for the winter. This would mean that the animals would go short again.

Victor had started his period of leadership with the best of intentions. The cost of replacing the generator would mean that the animals would not enjoy the more comfortable existence. Victor had intended to improve the relationships between Manor Farm and the other farms in the neighbourhood. Following the disaster with the generator, the surrounding farms had little faith in his ability to change Manor Farm.

Chapter XI

Victor was a Tamworth, a pig with principles. He was still optimistic about the future of Manor Farm despite the disaster with the generator. Although the other farms could see that Victor was trying to move in the right direction, they were taken aback by the subsequent ecological disaster of the generator. There was pressure on Victor to move forward and to be more enlightened.

Victor decided to talk to Michael and Margaret Pilkington about the management of Foxwood Farm. The pigs from Manor Farm had moved into Foxwood to "help" the Pilkingtons. Whilst there had been some resistance, the pigs brought with them some of the dogs, which so ably and heartlessly enforced the will of the pigs on Manor Farm. The Pilkingtons sat waiting for Victor to arrive. They looked nervously at each other. Over the past few years the arrival of the top pig meant that there was trouble of some sort: production needed to be increased, food allocations needed to be decreased, Foxwood's contribution to Manor Farm needed to be increased, or a combination of the three. In any event, it was never good news.

Victor arrived and sat down with Michael and Margaret. They soon realised that this was no normal visit. Victor opened by saying "these are times of great change and upheaval." Michael and Margaret were dumbstruck. They had no idea how this conversation would end. Was Victor planning on taking over Foxwood completely? Victor carried on "In the past, I and the other pigs have been very pleased to help you run this farm. Now the time has come for you to stand on your own two feet". The irony of a pig talking about standing on two feet was not lost to them. "I have decided that you should be given full responsibility for running Foxwood Farm. In the coming months we will make arrangements for the complete handover of responsibilities." Thus Victor agreed with the Pilkingtons that they would resume full ownership and control of Foxwood Farm. At first they were alarmed and confused; for many years they had been following the guidance of Manor Farm. However, as time went on they got used to the idea and eventually relished the thought of being fully responsible for what was after all their farm.

Soon the pigs and dogs left the farm and returned to live in Manor Farm. There was great rejoicing on Foxwood Farm as the humans and animals joined together to celebrate their freedom. The Pilkingtons got used to the new independence and there was a feeling of optimism on the farm.

Following the departure of the pigs, Foxwood Farm started to create its own trading relationships with local towns and villages. The people and animals on Foxwood Farm started to travel freely between their home and other farms towns and villages. Outsiders began to recognise Foxwood as an independent and friendly farm with which they could do business. The reputation of the Pilkingtons grew so much that they developed a trading agreement with Mr. Wordsworth of Beech Tree Farm. They agreed that they would share produce between themselves but they would also join together to sell their produce to third parties.

Pinchfield Farm, the farm adjacent to Manor Farm, had been divided between Manor Farm and Beech Tree Farm following the great storm several years before. Beech Tree had already given independence to half the farm under the ownership of Mr. Lawrence. This half had made great strides in mechanisation and productivity. Following the withdrawal from Foxwood Farm, there was great pressure on Victor to let go of their half of Pinchfield Farm. Victor decided to achieve a place in history by removing the dog patrols from the boundary between Pinchfield and Manor Farms. Animals on both sides responded to the withdrawal of the patrols by starting to demolish the barbed wire barrier. Small sections were left in place as a reminder of what it used to be like. As the fence was demolished, animals from both sides crossed the wire and greeted each other enthusiastically. Meanwhile, the pigs in Pinchfield farmhouse became very nervous. They tried to destroy all the evidence of the activities on Pinchfield Farm and eventually they fled to Manor Farm taking anything they could. Sometime later the animals found the remnants of the records kept by the pigs in the farmhouse. Although the majority of the records had been destroyed or removed it seemed evident that the records had been enormous. It looked like there had been a file on every animal and human on Pinchfield Farm and other farms as well. The animals agreed that the records would be locked away in the cellar and never looked at again.

After much discussion between Victor and Beech Tree Farm, Mr. Lawrence agreed to pay compensation to Manor Farm and take full responsibility for the whole of Pinchfield. The two halves had become very different. The half that had been run by Beech Tree Farm and then by Mr. Lawrence was a vibrant, happy place. The humans and animals were respected and treated fairly. On the other hand the half that was run by Manor Farm was run down and depressed. Animals and humans were downtrodden and wary of each other. Mr. Lawrence started to integrate the two halves. Firstly, he allowed complete mobility within the combined farm. Secondly, animals and humans were free to visit Beech Tree Farm and beyond. Thirdly, the working conditions formerly enjoyed by Mr. Lawrence's animals and humans were shared by all. Initially, this led to some shortages and a little resentment but eventually the halves started to work comfortably together. After several years following the merger they begin to look like one farm again. Both halves of Pinchfield Farm became part of the cooperation agreement with Foxwood. Other local farms joined in the agreement, leaving Manor Farm isolated and cut off from other farms.

Having lived through great changes, Mr. Lawrence decided to retire and was replaced by Mr. Honey, who took up residence in the old farm house in what used to be the Manor Farm controlled half of Pinchfield. He continued the full merger of the two halves of Pinchfield Farm.

The cooperation between Pinchfield, Beech Tree and Foxwood Farms grew blossomed. The farms shared experiences and expertise. They continued to sell, buy and sell to each other but they also developed more and more joint ventures to sell to third parties far and wide.

Having lost control of Foxwood and Pinchfield Farms, Victor concentrated on modernising Manor Farm. He started by renaming it Animal Farm once more. As the dogs died they were not replaced and their numbers were reduced. He reduced the stockpile of dynamite that had been accumulated to confront Pinchfield and Beech Tree Farms. This brought a sense of optimism to all the animals on Animal farm. They believed that the future was going to be better.

Not all the animals were in favour of the changes that had happened over the last couple of years. The pigs saw their importance dwindling and their lifestyle being threatened. Victor was destroying everything that they have worked for over the years. The pigs plotted to remove him.

Victor felt very tired after many years of running Animal Farm. He had overseen enormous changes during his lifetime. The two adjoining farms had been given to their rightful owners. Animal Farm itself was more open and optimistic. However, these changes had taken their toll. Victor felt older and weaker than he had ever felt before. The other pigs had noticed the change and decided that he should be replaced. They insisted that Victor resigned. Consequently they held an election which involved not just the pigs but all the animals on Animal Farm. Nonetheless, the choice was limited; whatever happened, a pig was going to be elected.

There were three challengers for the leadership. The favourite was Romeo, a Gloucestershire Old Spot, who was elected by a clear majority. The pigs and animals were confident about the future. Romeo vowed to transform the farm. No longer would the pigs led by Romeo decide what the farm was going to do in the future. It would be decided by market forces. If the market for potatoes was good, then the farm would increase potato growing and sell their stock; if the market for corn was good, then they would sell the corn. Again, the animals were confused. Franco had questioned the leadership of Napoleon, Ethelred questioned the leadership of Franco, Victor questioned the leadership with Ethelred, and now Romeo was telling them that they had been wrong in the past and they were moving in a new direction. This was very confusing for the animals. But, inevitably, the sheep bleated "Romeo knows best! Romeo knows best!" And so Animal Farm continued.

Chapter XII

Although there had been changes in the approach to managing Animal Farm, very little had been done to maintain the fabric of the buildings over the last few years. The barns, stables and outbuildings were in a terrible state. Paintwork was peeling, panels were missing and doors were hanging off their hinges. This allowed the rats to come and go as they pleased. In the original charter of Animal Farm it stated that no animal should hurt any other animal. Whilst this commandment, along with all the others, had been broken frequently over the years, the rats had been left alone. This was fine when they were small in number and food was plentiful but became much more of an issue when they were breeding in large numbers and food was scarce.

The pigs tried to control the number of rats but they were too slow and ineffective. The pigs then ordered the dogs to hunt and kill the rats but the rats were too fast, even for the dogs. The rats could enter and leave the buildings by what seemed like an endless number of entrances and the dogs were too large to follow them. There was a farm cat called Ebenezer, an old ginger tom, fat and slow. He just sat and looked as first the pigs and then the dogs tried to chase and catch the rats.

The pigs decided that something should be done. The original Seven Commandments that had been painted on the end of the barn included commandment number six "no animal shall kill any other animal". This commandment, like all the others, had been disregarded in the past and Romeo decided that it would be disregarded now. He arranged for rat poison to be delivered from the village and this was put in suitable locations around the barn and other areas. The intention was simply to kill off all the rats. However, they were too clever. They had had the run of the farm for so long that they had developed into a well-planned, structured and organised group. The word went around that there was poison and it should be avoided. Consequently the poison was completely ineffective. The rats continued to breed in great numbers and continued to help themselves to grain from the barn. Clearly something more drastic needed to be done. The pigs decided that they would need to introduce young healthy cats to deal with the rat problem.

They started with Peter, Augustus, and James. These were young and agile cats. Deliberately deprived of food, the cats were hungry and chased and killed the rats. They started to patrol the barn, grain store, hay loft and potato shed. They were so successful that Romeo decided to increase the numbers of cats from three to six and introduced three more cats - Henry, George, and Bill. In the past Squealer, Trumpet and, then, Clarion had come up with fictitious statements of the amount of grain produced each year. These figures were not helpful and did not contribute to what was an inadequate planning process. What was needed was an understanding of the amount of crops grown so that there was enough to go round and perhaps even some left to sell. The cats were not as intelligent as the pigs but they were clever and cunning. Because they spent so much time in and around the barn, the cats were given responsibility for tracking the grain. Subsequently, because they were so organised, they became responsible for tracking all the crops; and, then, were given responsibility for selling the grain, potatoes and other crops to the local farm shops.

They took over the responsibility for the tenders that Franco had completed dishonestly in the past. The cats were cunning. They manipulated the figures so that they could actually take some of the profits which they put into accounts they had created. Gradually the six cats became more confident. They reached the point where they could trade in other goods such as fruit and timber. Romeo not only supported the cats' involvement, but also encouraged the cats to trade with the local shops and other farms. He was very pleased to see that the cats were implementing the open market policy that he had proposed when he took over leadership of the farm. The cats were starting to become very wealthy. There were rumours that some pigs were taking a percentage and creating their own nest eggs. Meanwhile the lower animals were still not well off.

The cats grew richer and richer. They generated enough wealth to convert one of the outbuildings into their own comfortable cat house. They were joined by other clever and cunning cats. Using their growing wealth the cats arranged for the building of a bigger windmill. It was so large that it could supply ample electricity to Animal Farm. The power generated provided some creature comforts for the animals. There was enough spare capacity to enable the cats to sell electricity to neighbouring farms. Using the money from the sale of electricity the cats bought a brand new tractor and tools for the farm. This made life a little easier for the animals.

Neighbours including Beech Tree Farm were so impressed that they entered into agreements with the cats. Jointly they built windmills to generate and sell electricity on their farms. Eventually, the cats were involved with a dozen farms, each with a large windmill producing electricity for itself and its neighbours. This arrangement worked well. The cats were bringing wealth into Animal Farm, eventually having enough wealth to rebuild the barn.

Meanwhile Romeo was starting to lose popularity. The other animals were not convinced that the cats should control the wealth of the farm. He ordered the dissolution of the meetings of the pigs. The pigs objected but Romeo ordered the remaining dogs to impose his decision. He informed all the animals that from now on he would be President Romeo. He appointed Lancelot, a loyal pig, as his Deputy. A group of the more traditional pigs started to plot against Romeo. One day Romeo made a surprise announcement of his resignation. When he became leader he was held in high esteem and optimism. When Romeo left office, he was widely unpopular with most of the pigs and the rest of the animals. He left the presidency in the hands of his chosen successor, the Deputy President, Lancelot.

Lancelot, a British Landrace pig, was slimmer and fitter than any pig that had gone before him. Lancelot was duly elected unopposed and once elected he took over control of the farm. He was seen around the farm occasionally not just on special occasions and he restored weekly meetings. He presented a friendly face to Animal Farm and the rest of the world. The pigs felt that Lancelot was an improvement on Victor because he was reverting back to an older style of leadership.

Lancelot gathered all the animals together for a meeting in the barn. He said that he had been listening to the wishes of all the animals and he declared he would be Life President of Animal Farm!

After a while, Lancelot started to feel threatened by the accumulated wealth which was not under the direct control of the pigs. Lancelot accused one of the cats, Augustus, of corruption and fraud. Augustus was tried by a collection of the pigs that were presented with irrefutable evidence that he was guilty of the charges. Consequently they found Augustus guilty. There was no doubt that the pigs had been instructed to choose this verdict. The cat's wealth was taken away from him and he was banished to a farm in the North of England. One of the other cats, James, was visiting Beech Tree Farm when he suddenly fell ill. A few days later, he died from some mysterious feline virus. At the time it was said that James had died of natural causes, but the suspicion remained that he had been poisoned in some way. Following the trial of Augustus and the death of James, the cats and pigs lived uncomfortably side by side.

Generally, the neighbouring farms were contented with the partnerships with the cats to produce and supply electricity. However, they were concerned that in the longer term there would be problems between the pigs and the cats that would endanger their energy supplies. They were approached by an agent of Lancelot who suggested that they could give up the partnership with the cats and join in a partnership with the pigs on Animal Farm. After all, the cats were from Animal Farm and were generating the wealth on its behalf. One by one, the farm owners gave up their partnership with the cats and aligned themselves with Lancelot and the pigs. The cats still had financial interests but there was a shift of ownership from the cats to the pigs.

Lancelot felt more in control of Animal Farm than he had done for some time. He announced elections would be introduced as part of the changes on Animal Farm. Subsequently, these were held and Lancelot was elected unopposed. He declared that he would continue to be Life President of Animal Farm.

Chapter XIII

There followed a time of great optimism. The cats had been providing a source of wealth for themselves and all the animals on the farm. The lower animals continued to enjoy some of this financial success. Manor Farm had been renamed Animal Farm and all the animals felt more content with their lot. The removal of barriers with other farms led to travelling between farms becoming commonplace. People and animals came to look at Animal Farm. The animals themselves went to visit other farms. This was particularly true for young animals that went on visits, learned new techniques and expanded their horizons. In the past, this would have been prohibited. Now there was a high degree of mobility with little control by Lancelot and the other pigs. It was accepted that the animals would travel freely but would always return to Animal Farm. There was no need to create ties to ensure that they returned.

This openness created a sense of well-being in the animals. Added to this was the increase in their standard of living because of the wealth generated by the cats. Whilst Romeo was leader, much of the wealth generated was held by the cats, although there were allegations of corruption and bribery with the pigs. Lancelot ensured that the wealth generated was divided amongst all the animals. They saw an increase in their food allowances a reduction in their working week and an overall improvement in their standard of living and accommodation.

In this new atmosphere of happiness and optimism, animals got together to enjoy this new openness. One group was a collection of hens who gathered in their spare moments to socialise and chat. The five hens Anna, Tanya, Helena, Katya, and Natasha started to sing together. Initially they sang for their own amusement. It became known on the farm that the hens were entertaining and so they were asked to sing for the rest of the animals. They named themselves Hen Party. As they entertained more and more their reputation grew until even surrounding farms had heard of their existence. They were tolerated by Lancelot and the rest of the pigs as a diversion from the day-to-day monotony of the farm.

Hen Party started by singing well-known nursery rhymes, songs taken from old books in the farmhouse and also one or two songs that they had put together themselves. One day the pigeons told Hen Party that they could just about recollect the words and music of words of Beasts of England taught to them by their grandparents. Hen Party learned the words and tune and practised the song. One Sunday as the animals gathered in the barn at the end of the weekly meeting, Hen Party stood up and moved to the front and broke into a rousing rendition of Beasts of England. Suddenly inside the barn was pandemonium. Two of the hens, Katya and Natasha, managed to flee the barn and ran to Beech Tree Farm for safety. Three of the hens were apprehended by the dogs under command of the pigs. The three hens, Anna, Tanya, and Helena, were placed in a shed isolated from the other animals and guarded by two of the dogs.

After being left alone like this for three days they were taken by the dogs to the farmhouse where they were put on trial in front of three of the pigs acting as judges. The chair of the pigs stated that the hens had been arrested because they had performed a banned song and this was acting as a destabilising influence on the rest of Animal Farm. The three hens from Hen Party had little chance to explain themselves or their actions. They were taken back to the shed to await the judgement of the three pigs. Meanwhile there had been a protest from the other animals on the farm and indeed from animals on other farms far and wide. It was felt that the hens should not be prosecuted for reviving some of the old values inherent in Beasts of England.

All the animals thought that the three hens would be given a warning and told not to sing such songs again. However there was a belief that Lancelot was instructing the pigs to find the three hens guilty and give them a severe sentence. After two days of deliberation, three pigs found the hens guilty of sedition and sentenced them to long-term imprisonment. The two hens that had fled were found guilty in their absence. One of the hens Anna, whose clutch of eggs was about to hatch, was allowed to go free. On release she scurried off to look after her chicks.

The two remaining hens did not blame Anna for wanting to be with her chicks. However, Tanya and Helena were concerned that they would be punished further. In times gone by, they would have been sentenced to death and savaged by the dogs. This was no longer the case but there was a feeling that they could be sent far away to another farm somewhere in the North of England or beyond. Two days later a van arrived. Tanya and Helena were grabbed by the pigs, forced into a crate, and thrown into the back of the van. The van drove away and Tanya and Helena were never seen again.

Lancelot had been responsible for an improvement in the standard of living for all the animals on the farm. But now there were questions about his conduct in office. There was concern about Lancelot's relations with the cats. Lancelot complained that the cats were opposing Animal Farm and this was orchestrated by Pinch Field Farm and the cats that had left Animal Farm into self-imposed exile. The lower animals, whilst enjoying new liberties and a better standard of living were concerned about their freedom. No animal was allowed to speak out against President Lancelot and his pigs. The rest of the pigs and lower animals were not allowed to show dissension.

Epilogue

Animal Farm had seen many changes over the years. Some animals claim that they remembered the early Manor Farm. Some animals even claimed that they remembered the Joneses but they were long gone and a distant memory. Since then there had been the rebellion when the animals took over the farm and renamed it Animal Farm. Subsequently the pigs took leadership and ran the farm. Conflict with other farms had included the taking over and relinquishing of Foxwood Farm and the occupation and subsequent withdrawal of Pinchfield Farm. The rivalry with Beech Tree Farm had created an atmosphere of uncertainty over the years.

There had been periods of happiness and sadness. There had been periods of optimism and pessimism. Now Manor Farm was once again Animal Farm. The lower animals were fairly content although still largely impoverished. Opening up the farm meant that people could visit the farm including a mobile grocery van and even a mobile library. This gave those animals able to read an opportunity to discover a wider world through literature. The pigs and other animals were allowed and even encouraged to visit other farms to learn up-to-date farming methods,

But Animal Farm was undecided and unsure about the present and what the future would bring. The trial and imprisonment of Hen Party had left the animals wondering how much control they had over their own destiny. The continued rivalry between the pigs that ran the farm and the cats who manipulated the finances continued. This was the most worrying aspect of all. The pigs and cats co-existed side-by-side but nobody knew how long this uneasy cooperation would last.

The power of the cats, based on their financial acumen and success, was also under threat. Neighbouring farms were going through a bad patch and were less able or willing to pay high prices for their electricity. The windmills that had been a source of regular income for years were no longer giving such large rewards. Whilst the cats were not penniless, they were not in the comfortable position that they had been for years and years.

Both the pigs and the cats felt threatened by change and also by each other. The differences between the pigs and cats could easily escalate into conflict. These differences were typified by Lancelot accusing the cats of fraud and treason. Consequently, some of the cats decided to leave Animal Farm and live on the neighbouring farms that welcomed them. One such cat was George. He fled Animal Farm and was given a place to live at

Pinchfield Farm. Whilst there, he openly spoke out against Lancelot and the other pigs on Manor Farm. In reply, Lancelot declared that George was a traitor and his wealth was confiscated by Lancelot and Manor Farm. Not long after it was reported that George had died in mysterious circumstances. There were rumours that he had been killed by an agent of Lancelot or he had taken his own life in despair.

Lancelot was determined to maintain his stronghold on Animal Farm. He decreed that all animals, especially cats, should declare any interest they had in foreign farms. Furthermore, they should declare any joint ventures that involved Animal Farm. Punishment for non-declaration would be severe. All animals lived in fear of recrimination.

The pigs' power which was still based largely on intimidation and threats was being questioned by the lower animals, the cats and the outside world. To reinforce their position Lancelot ordered that a message should be painted on the new barn:

'All animals are equal,
but some animals are more equal than others,
and no animals are more equal than the pigs'

It had been a long time since the rebellion. All the animals on the farm had been born long after Mr. Jones had been chased off Animal Farm. Most animals could barely remember what the rebellion was all about. The animals knew that they were more comfortable now than their predecessors had been years ago but they were anxious. What little they had could so easily be taken away.

Dramatis Personæ

The Farms
Manor Farm
Originally owned by Mr. and Mrs. Jones, Manor Farm was taken in the Animal Rebellion and renamed Animal Farm. Later, Napoleon, the pig leader, renamed it Manor Farm once more.

Foxwood Farm
Owned by Mr. Pilkington and his wife Gladys, Foxwood Farm was a large, neglected, old-fashioned farm. It was situated alongside Manor Farm.

Pinchfield Farm
Owned by Mr. Frederick, and situated the other side of Manor Farm, Pinchfield Farm was smaller and better kept.

Beech Tree Farm
Beyond Pinchfield was Beech Tree Farm which was wealthy and well-maintained. It was owned by Mr. Verity.

Lone Tree Farm, Maple Farm, New Farm, and South Farm
All involved in the biennial Farm Gala.

Pig Leaders (in order)

Napoleon

A large, rather fierce-looking Berkshire boar, not much of a talker, but with a reputation for getting his own way.

Franco

Another Berkshire boar, loyal deputy and successor to Napoleon.

Ethelred

An old Large White pig, keen on traditions but past his best.

Victor

A Tamworth with red-gold hair who appeared softer and kinder than his predecessors.

Romeo

A Gloucestershire Old Spot, the first pig elected by all the animals.

Lancelot

A British Landrace, Lancelot was slimmer and fitter than any pig that had gone before him. Romeo's Deputy and chosen successor.

Other Pigs

Alfred
A mature pig chosen by Franco to design and build the potato picker.

Clarion
The spokespig for Ethelred. He replaced Trumpet when he was forced to resign.

Columbus
Trusted by Franco, Columbus negotiated a settlement during the gunpowder dispute.

Minimus
A pig with a talent for writing poetry and songs. Loyal to Napoleon.

Old Major
The prize Middle White boar who shared his vision of a new world for animals free from oppression. He passed away soon after.

Snowball
A more vivacious pig than Napoleon, quicker in speech and more inventive. He was denounced as a traitor and chased off Animal Farm by Napoleon's dogs.

Squealer
A small fat pig with very round cheeks. He was a brilliant talker and the mouthpiece for Napoleon.

Tom, Dick, Harry, and Jack
Distinctive Oxford Sandy and Black pigs all from the same litter; bought by Mr. Verity for Beech Tree Farm.

Trumpet
The spokespig for Franco, he replaced Squealer.

The Animals
Benjamin, the donkey

Bluebell, Jessie, and Pincher, the three dogs

Boxer and Clover, the two cart-horses

Ebenezer, the old farm cat

Mollie, the foolish, pretty white mare

Moses, the tame raven

Muriel, the white goat

The Cats
Augustus, Bill, George, Henry, James, and Peter.
Recruited by Romeo to control the rats. The cats took responsibility for the finances of Manor Farm.

Hen Party
Anna, Tanya, Helena, Katya, and Natasha
A group of singing hens.

The Humans

Mr. Arbuthnot
A solicitor in Mr. Whymper's office.

Mr. Bartholomew
A trusted customer of Mr. Verity.

Nicholas Handy
A farmhand on Manor Farm who crept into Pinchfield Farm to steal the designs of their machinery.

Mr. Honey
Bought Pinchfield Farm from Mr. Lawrence and continued the merger.

Ted James
A trusted farmhand of Mr. Verity on Beech Tree Farm.

Mr. Lawrence
A distant relative of Mr. Frederick. He started to merge the two halves of Pinchfield Farm.

Andrew Newton
A Beech Tree farmhand sent by Mr. Verity to spy on Manor Farm.

Michael and Margaret Pilkington
Son and daughter-in-law of the Pilkingtons. They inherited Foxwood Farm.

George Thomas
A designer of farm equipment.

Percival Verity
Brother of Mr. Verity, the owner of Beech Tree Farm.

Mr. Whymper
A solicitor living in Willingdon, the local market town.

Mr. Wordsworth
Bought Beech Tree Farm from Mr. Verity.

Made in the USA
Monee, IL
23 November 2020

49083207R00075